Jailbait Jasmine

By S L Williams

Chapter 1

I'm sitting next to my fiancé once again, questioning if this is where I should be? Is it fair to marry someone when I knowingly can't give her my whole heart because it belongs to another? Or maybe, I'm feeling out of sorts because our wedding day is less than six months away, and I know that once I say I do, I'll have to give up my dream of finding and reconciling with Jasmine, a girl who I always have and always will love. I don't take marriage lightly, and I know that once I say I do, that's it. I couldn't leave my wife, even to be with the love of my life, because I'd have to be a man and honor my commitment. A man's word should stand for something, and for me, mine does.

Besides, seconds have turned into minutes, minutes into hours, hours into days, months, and now years.

Jasmine's been out of my life for almost five years now, but I still crave her soft sensual touch, long to kiss her sweet tender lips, and I would do or give anything to have her in my arms and bed again. I want to feel once more like I did when we made sweet passionate love for the first and only time all those years ago.

I know it's crazy, but I can still feel her warm, soft hand gently caressing my manhood in such a timid inexperienced way that I knew she'd never done it before and feeling the sheer excitement of knowing without a shadow of a doubt that I would be her first. I can even hear myself asking her if she was sure because we'd never meant for things to go that far, but we eventually gave in to our undeniable love and heartfelt passion. However, I guess for her, it was just for a season, although I wanted it to be for a lifetime. She was the woman I wanted to marry and have to bear my children.

Feeling a somewhat forceful shake on my shoulder, I turned around quickly to see my fiance, Leah, staring at me, "Hey, earth to Julian, where were you a minute ago?"

"What do you mean?

"I mean, the cake designer tried to get your attention a couple of times, but you seemed to be null and void! What's gotten into you lately? Your body is here, but your mind is rarely present! This blank disconnected stare is getting to be ridiculous, and I'm tired of you embarrassing me. So when she returns, can you at least pretend to be a little more enthusiastic? You need to get over whatever is bothering you, and you need to get over it now!"

"Hey, I'm sorry! It's not because I'm not excited, but you already know that at the end of the day, it'll be whichever cake you and your mom decide on, and that's fine with me."

"Julian, that's not true!"

"Yeah, it is, but it doesn't matter to me because you both have excellent taste. Your mom is an interior decorator, and you being a highly sought after photojournalist, definitely have an eye for the dramatic. And both of your homes are beautifully decorated, so I have full faith in you guys to pick a cake that will wow everyone."

Slightly smiling, she quickly took a sip of water and leaned forward in her seat, "Okay, as long as you put it like that, I forgive you."

As soon as the designer returned with samples, I tried hard to be more engaged, but to be honest, my heart wasn't quite in it, although I wanted it to be. I wanted to be happy and feel excited, but instead, I felt anxious and somewhat depressed. And I didn't think it was normal for a bridegroom to feel this way.

"Okay, guys, have we decided on a design? And here are the samples that you all requested. The first one is a yellow cake with a raspberry filling and frosting. The second is a white cake, with a cream cheese filling and a sweet lemon frosting, and the last, but certainly not least, is a pink champagne cake with a strawberry mousse filling on some layers and rosewater mousse on others. It also has a pink champagne buttercream frosting. And either one will be covered in fondant to achieve the glamorous glasslike finish that you all requested.

After sampling the cakes, I was unshakably sold on the pink champagne sample because it was moist and delicious. And I was incredibly surprised that Leah didn't like it as well, nor did she particularly like either of the other two that were also quite good.

Seeing the look of sheer frustration on the cake designer, Carol's face, as she cleared the table, I could feel her pain. She was tired of Leah, and so was I because this poor woman had gone through this three times with us before. And I'm sure that she was beginning to wonder if the $12,000.00 she was being paid for our cake and cupcakes, and $2,000.00, for my groom's cake, a simple chocolate cake shaped like a football field with edible white goalposts, turfgrass, and tiny footballs was worth it. Money isn't everything!

It was going to be such an expensive cake because, for some reason, my fiancée wanted the flowers to be airbrushed with gold leaf, something that doesn't even have a distinctive taste, but that's what she wanted. And her parents were all too happy to pay for it. I think their sole mission in life is to cater to Leah and give her anything she wants, even if it's outrageous and borders on being absurd.

We both come from well to do families, but my family isn't stuck on status, whereas hers is all about image and what others think about them. I don't get it, but that's who they are. Her family owns a hugely successful software company, and they spoil her rotten. And I think that's the only thing that she and Jasmine have in common other than both being female. Because she comes from a very wealthy family too, but she didn't act spoiled at all, although she got pretty much anything she wanted, as well. She's her parents' little princess, and they would do anything in the world for her, and so would I.

Yet, she never exhibited that superior attitude that Leah sometimes displays. But Jasmine was most assuredly very confident and a fierce go-getter. If she wanted something, she went for it, and for a long time, she wanted me and never tried to hide it. But then her parents decided to expand their lucrative business and moved away to an undisclosed destination, and she never tried to get in touch with me, not even once.

I'd called her every few hours after they moved, but she never picked up. I kept calling for days until, eventually,

her number was no longer in service, and that
devastated me because that was my only lifeline to her.
So for months, I walked around in a daze, struggling to
come to terms with what had happened. I was
devastated because my entire world had crumbled, and
I felt lost! Because when she left, she took my hopes
and dreams for our future together with her.

Truthfully, there are still nights that I vividly dream about
her being in bed lying next to me, only to wake up
suddenly and discover that it was just a dream. She
wasn't there, and my heart would ache all over again.
This girl has left a mark on me that time, nor distance
has managed to erase or even lessen. It's a mark that
has penetrated the very core of who I am because
Jasmine is and always will be an intricate part of me.

"Come on, Julian, our appointment is over, and Carol
has another couple waiting, so we'll have to come back
in a couple of weeks."

"Okay, but why don't we include your mom next time, so
that way, we can go on and make a decision. As I said
earlier, I'm sure I'll be more than satisfied with whatever
cake you two decide on, so I'll more or less keep my
mouth closed. The designer already has the
dimensions, so it'll fit on your great grandmother's
antique cake stand, so it's just a matter of choosing the
style and flavor. And we already know that it has to be
round.

"Well, I want your input, but you know my mom would love to help us pick out a cake. But are you sure it's okay with you?" Looking at me intently, she grabbed her purse off the table and put it on her shoulder as we prepared to leave.

"Yeah, I'm sure, and besides, your mom wants a more active role in planning the wedding anyway, so this will make her happy, and it'll make you happy too."

"Okay, well, it's settled. I'll call and let my mom know."

Upon entering the car, she called her immediately, and I could hear the excitement in her mothers' voice over the phone, "Okay, Leah, we're going to find y'all the perfect cake, and I guess I need to be thanking Julian."

"Yeah, mom, it was all his idea, and I'll tell him what you said. I'll talk to you later."

"Alright, as you probably heard, she loves the idea and said thank you. Maybe, this will be a bonding experience for the two of you because it would be nice if you guys could become closer. Since there's always a little hint tension when you all are around each other, and I want that to change."

"Yeah, well, your mom only wants you to be happy, and that's as it should be. But sometimes, I think she wonders if I'm the right man for the job."

"Julian, she likes you, but she questions if I have your whole heart, and you have to admit that you can become a little disengaged at times. She and my father just want me to be happy, just like your parents want happiness for you. I know they still have doubts too, and your sister certainly isn't my biggest fan. She thinks I'm a spoiled, selfish, self-absorbed little bitch who's all wrong for you, and considering how distant you act towards me sometimes, I guess I can understand why she feels that way."

"Well, I'm going to make an effort to do better all the way around because I realize that I've been a little distant and lost in my thoughts lately. So I'm working hard on me."

"Okay, I'm glad to hear you say that because this is our time, and I think we can be happy together. Neither one of us has kids, so we can start our little clan of Petersons in a year or two. I'd love to give you a son, or a beautiful little girl, who I can picture now." Smiling and closing her eyes briefly, she reached out to hold my hand. "Or perhaps, I'll give you both."

I cared deeply for her, but I knew in my heart that I'd never love her or anyone else as I love Jasmine. My love for her is on an entirely different level, and that's a level that no one else will ever reach or come close to touching. She's undoubtedly the love of my life, but years have passed, and I have to find a way to move on with my life. Besides, it's as though she's disappeared from the face of the earth. I've been online searching for Jasmine Danielle Darrington consistently, but I can't find her, and I feel incredibly guilty for continuing my search, even after I got engaged. I know it's not right, but I think I could move forward easier if I only knew why she never got in touch with me. Maybe talking to her face to face would give me some sense or measure of desperately needed closure.

It wouldn't stop me from loving her, but maybe I could, at the very least, understand why she wouldn't take or return my calls. If it's because she'd met and fallen in love with someone else, I'd be hurt, but I'd at least have the answer that I felt cheated out of. The not knowing was haunting and consuming me, so I spent a lot of sleepless nights lying in bed, wondering why. And I'm not proud of it, but some of those times, I was lying next to Leah or other girls longing to experience once again how Jasmine made me feel. But unfortunately, I've never felt that way since we were together.

"Hey, please drop me off at my apartment, so I can get my car because I'm not going back to work today. I think I'll go and hang out with my friend, Amy, for a while. And maybe, we can get a mani-pedi after a late lunch."

"Okay, well, tell her I said hello."

After dropping her off, I headed back to my office, where I work for my family's engineering company, Peterson United, as vice-president. My father is the CEO, and my mom is president. We all have degrees in finance and business management from the University of Virginia.

It's a very profitable company, and we take pride in carrying on my great, great grandparents' legacy. My sister, Cathy, is a college student majoring in business with a minor in psychology and will be graduating next spring. Then, she'll be coming on board in the human resources department. We're a tight-knit clan and tremendously proud of our heritage and strive hard to preserve our legacy because we're determined to leave a solid foundation for future generations, just as our forefathers did for us.

As soon as I entered the building, I saw my father standing in the hallway, motioning for me, and walked over quickly.

"Hey, Dad, what's up?"

"Son, your mother and I were wondering if you and Leah would like to join us for dinner this evening? Cathy's free, and she's coming, but her boyfriend has to work late."

"Yeah, well, that sounds good to me, but Leah is hanging out with a friend, so it'll only be the four of us, and I'm looking forward to it."

"Okay, but are things alright between you and Leah?"

"Yeah, things are fine."

"Well, I sure hope so, but if you ever need to talk, I'm always here."

"I know, and I appreciate it, but we're okay."

"Aright, well, your mom and sister are going to meet us at the restaurant around six, and it's right up the street, so if it's okay with you, we can go from here."

"Sure, that's fine, and this way, I'll have a couple of hours to get a little work done."

I went to my office, but I couldn't focus on paperwork because I couldn't get Jasmine off my mind. She had a milestone birthday coming up soon, and we'd made a promise to spend it together. It was supposed to be the day that we would wed and start our lives as husband and wife. And I couldn't help but wonder if that promise ever crosses her mind? Does she ever sit and think or dream about me too?

I often sit and daydream about times gone by. Jasmine's parents are my godparents, and my parents are hers. So for as long as I can remember, I've known her. My sister Cathy and she aren't quite three months apart, and I remember when they were born because I'd turned five. And I can vaguely recall my parents bringing my sister home, and months later, we were going to my godparents' house to see their new baby. And I can also remember thinking, she's even smaller than my little sister, and she probably cries a lot too.

Our parents have been best friends dating back to college, so our families spent countless weekends and holidays together. Jasmine is their only child, and I viewed her just as I did, Cathy. She was a little sister to me, and I felt extremely protective of her. If anyone bothered her, they had to answer to me. And she and Cathy were best friends and kept me on my toes. They were both pretty, popular girls who garnered a lot of attention, and I was the big brother from hell who looked out for them, checking guys if I felt like I needed to.

Growing up, Jasmine loved to tag along, mimicking whatever I was doing. She's the princess type, but she'd get wet and dirty if I did, although she hated it. If I dug up worms, she wanted to dig them up too. Even though it was pretty apparent that she was disgusted, by the way, she always frowned when they came wriggling out the ground. But she was like my shadow, and I couldn't turn for her. And our parents thought it was cute that she wanted to follow and emulate her big brother. Everyone also knew she had a crush on me, but we were so young that it spoke of pure childhood innocence. We were encouraged to act like big brother and little sister, but she'd bat her eyes at me and blow me kisses, and everybody would laugh.

However, as the months and years passed us by, our relationship started to change. Jasmine had always been a pretty little girl, but she grew into an incredibly beautiful, sexy, confident, young woman, who looked and dressed like a fashion model, and I couldn't help but take notice. She was gorgeous, and her body was banging because she stood 5ft. 6 inches tall and was undoubtedly 36,24, 36, and weighed about 120 pounds or so. She also had long dark hair and eyes, and her skin is the color of light caramel. And I found her sexy and appealing as hell and spent a lot of time daydreaming and fantasizing about her.

That was when our parents didn't think her crush on me was that cute anymore, and the time we spent together started to concern them because we were always whispering and smiling at each other. And they didn't want us left alone under any circumstances, nor was she allowed to wear a bikini or bathing suit when she came over to swim, as she had in the past. She had to wear swim shorts and a tee-shirt, but when she'd get out of the pool, I could still see her perfect body through her clinging wet clothes. It would look like she'd been in a wet t-shirt contest, and I'd feel the tinges of being sexually excited.

However, at the very beginning of my attraction to her, I tried hard to fight it. Because we'd been encouraged to act like siblings, and that's how I'd always thought of her. But that started to change because I found myself jealous as hell of any guy who I thought liked her. And all of my friends found her attractive, and I'd catch them checking her out. But I'd tell them that she was much too young for them, and I'd hurt anyone who bothered her. And being that I was well over six ft tall and weighed 215 PDS, with no fat whatsoever, they left her alone because I towered over them, and they knew I meant what I said. I didn't play around when it came to Cathy or Jasmine! And the fact that I was a heavily recruited defensive tackle on the football team didn't hurt.

However, a severe knee injury ended my football career in the last game of my senior year. Thank goodness, it was in the state championship game, and we won the title. So I look back at that time in my life fondly, even though I had to have surgery and was out of commission for quite some time. And Jasmine would figure out a way to come and see me every day, if only for a brief moment, and that was the highlight of my day. Because just seeing her beautiful face made everything that I had to go through more bearable. Not to mention, she was my biggest cheerleader during my recovery. She'd text me words of encouragement every morning along with her picture, and I loved that.

"Hey, son, where were you a minute ago? I knocked on your door because your secretary isn't at her desk, but after you didn't answer, I was beginning to think you'd forgotten about dinner and had left. What's going on with you? You seem a little distant and distracted lately."

"It's nothing! I'm fine!"

"Okay, well, it's time for us to go eat. Your mother and sister are already at the restaurant, so let's go because, as you know, those two lovely ladies become impatient quickly if we're late.

As soon as we made it and walked in, I spotted my mom and sister in a small secluded room, and we were promptly escorted to their table and seated quickly.

"Hey, Cathy and I were waiting on you guys, so we haven't ordered anything yet. Do you all want to order an appetizer?"

"Yeah, mom, let's order several to share because I'm starving. The only thing I've eaten today was wedding cake samples." Chuckling, I pointed to my stomach when I heard it growling.

"And big brother, speaking of wedding cake, where's it all about me, Leah?"

"Well, Leah is hanging out with her friend, Amy."

The waitress came and took our appetizer and drink orders for bang-bang shrimp, crispy calamari, and spring rolls. We also ordered iced tea for everybody because Cathy was still too young to drink legally; however, her twenty-first birthday was fast approaching.

"Okay, Julian, what's going on between you and Leah because mom, dad, and I feel that you're having second thoughts about your upcoming wedding. You most definitely don't seem like a man anxiously awaiting his big day. And for the past couple of months, you've seemed a little off, but I can't quite put my finger on it." Gently tapping her fingers on the table, she peered at me through squinted eyes.

"Come on, Cathy, I know you don't think Leah's right for me, but we're getting married in a matter of months. So, please try to establish a closer relationship with her for my sake."

As soon as the waiter came with our appetizers and drinks, we cut off our conversation mid-air and placed our orders, continuing our conversation as soon as he left.

"I know she can be a bit self-centered at times, but she's not a bad person. We all have our shortcomings, and I happen to care about her."

"Yeah, big brother, and I care about the guy who just brought us our food, but I don't want to spend my life with him. You always say you care about her, but I've never once heard you say that you're in love with her. Are you sure that Leah is the right woman for you? Is she who you want to spend your life with? It would be much better to break an engagement than knowingly enter into a marriage that's all wrong for you. But knowing Leah, she'd sue you for breach of promise! Do you love her like a man should love a woman, who he's about to marry?"

She'd certainly managed to put me on the spot, and my parents were staring at me with questioning looks waiting for an answer. But thankfully, the waiter came back surprisingly quick with our food, and I was the recipient of a much-appreciated reprieve because I didn't want to answer that question. Cathy was minoring in psychology, and she was undeniably good at psychoanalyzing and interrogating people.

Ignoring her questions, I cut into my steak immediately, "Wow, this steak is a perfect medium-well, and mom, your dish looks good too. Please let me try your swordfish."

"Of course, you can."

I did, and it was delicious."

We went on to discuss other things, and I was glad the interrogation by my little sister was over because her questions had made me feel uncomfortable. I cared about Leah, and I loved her in a way, but I wasn't necessarily in love with her. Getting married was her idea, and I said okay because I feel this is as deep as I'm ever going to feel for anyone other than Jasmine.

Chapter 2

After dinner, I went home to my big empty house, looked at my inviting bed, and dove in headfirst. Leah stayed over occasionally, but we'd made a pact to limit sleepovers. Even though we're both grown, our parents didn't necessarily approve of us shacking-up, and to be honest, I wasn't too particular about it either. And when she did stay over, we didn't always engage in sex.

It took me a while to fall asleep because I couldn't get Jasmine off of my mind, and I found myself reliving special moments in our forbidden relationship. We often pretended to be dating other people to fool our parents into letting their guards down. I had a make-believe girlfriend named Tina, who my parents wanted to meet, and she had a make-believe boyfriend named Phillip, who was just a friend of hers, who'd pick her up and bring her to meet me.

We ran that game for months and would go to the movies or out to dinner in a nearby town. However, after a while, my father caught on because a friend of his mentioned seeing us out together. And he busted my ass about it big time! He said boy, "Don't end up in jail fooling around with Jasmine! She's a lovely young lady, but she's much too young for you, and you know it. So please don't make a stupid misstep and get your ass locked up because that's what will happen! Don't you dare touch that girl, and I mean that! But of course, his rhetoric fell on deaf ears. We just worked harder to disguise our relationship, so we turned to Cathy to help us.

The next couple of weeks flew by, and before I knew it, we were back at the bakery with Leah's mom, who was excited that we'd included her in our quest to find what Leah would see as the perfect wedding cake. She'd been beaming when we picked her up, and that made it all worthwhile.

And I took a backseat and kept my mouth shut, as I'd promised Leah. And let them choose the cake they wanted, which turned out to be a six-tier, shimmering, iridescent white cake with elements of pearls and diamonds, with gold flowers cascading from the top to the base with stairs leading two ways to cupcakes. They also chose lavender mousse for the layers and rosewater buttercream as the frosting. It was a beautiful cake, although it wasn't necessarily my taste because it was a little too feminine for me. But she and her mom were happy, and I was okay with it because I still had the grooms' cake that I wanted. And besides, it tasted good but not as good as the pink champagne cake.

I like Leah's parents, but there are moments that our relationship feels a little strained and forced. I treated their daughter exceptionally well, but her parents wanted her to be the center of my universe like she is theirs because she's their only child. But unfortunately, no matter how hard I tried to give her that, Jasmine still occupied an enormous amount of that space.

I haven't seen her in years, yet I still crave the sweet, passionate, innocent kisses that we shared every chance we could. We'd make out if the opportunity presented itself, but we weren't having sex because I knew she wasn't ready, and I was okay with that. Because I enjoyed being with Jasmine with her clothes on, way more than I ever did being another girl with hers' off! So it was about her, not sex, because sex was something that I could've gotten any time I wanted it from countless girls all too willing to give it to me anytime and anywhere.

"Julian, Leah, told me that it was your idea to let me help choose the cake, so I want to say thank you personally. Because helping my daughter pick out a wedding cake means the world to me."

"Mrs. Jones, you're more than welcome. I told Leah, you both have excellent taste, and I mean that. It's a beautiful cake, and I'm sure the wedding gown that you help her choose will be equally as beautiful."

"Well, thank you, and I'm going to invite your parents over for dinner sometime soon. That way, we can all become better acquainted." Smiling and reaching out, she hugged me.

"Yes, mam, I think that would be nice. So whenever you set a date, just let me know, and I'll tell my parents."

"Alright, well, I'll discuss it with Frank, and we'll work out all the details."

"Okay, I'm looking forward to it, and I'm sure my family will be happy to come."

"Julian, it's a shame that we haven't all spent more time together. Our children are getting married, and we'll soon be family." Reaching out, she hugged me again.

When we went to take Leah's mom home, her father was there, so I went in to speak and found him in the family room watching t.v, but he quickly muted it and reached out to shake my hand.

"Hey, son, it's good to see you, so come on in and have a seat. You need to come over more often to hang out and watch a game with me. And I'll put some steaks on the grill, and maybe we can throw back a couple of beers."

"Yes, sir, I will, and it's nice to see you too. And I'm looking forward to hanging out sometime soon."

I only stayed for twenty minutes or so and picked up Chinese food on my way home. When I got there, I sat down to eat and pulled out old pictures of Jasmine when she was head cheerleader and captain of the dance team. She was extremely popular and outgoing and had excess energy to spare.

I also looked at pictures from Christmas and birthday celebrations, and that reminded me that Cathy's birthday was in a few weeks, and I needed to find her the perfect gift. She's a great kid sister, and I wanted her twenty-first birthday present to be unique. She'd mentioned seeing a gold bracelet a few weeks ago that she liked a lot, and I decided it would be the perfect gift because I could have it engraved.

But thinking about buying her a bracelet also brought back memories of buying one for Jasmine for her sixteenth birthday. I was a college student, but my parents gave me a relatively generous allowance every month, along with a credit card for incidentals. And for a couple of months, I saved my food money to buy Jasmine an expensive bracelet by eating in the cafeteria and ramen noodles. I'd managed to save $2,000.00 for the charm bracelet, but I also decided to give her an inexpensive engagement ring that cost an additional $3,000.00. So I decided to put it all on my credit card to earn cash-back and then pay it off quickly because I already had $2,000.00 of it. I planned to disguise the ring as a charm, so no one would know that she had it. And she had so much jewelry that I surmised no one would even notice the bracelet anyway. It would be strictly between Cathy and us, but even she didn't know about the engagement ring. Because if by some remote chance anyone did find out, I didn't want her to be held responsible for not telling what I'd done because defying our parents was solely on me.

But as fate would have it, my mom, for the first time, actually looked at and questioned my credit card purchases. Even though I'd already paid $2,000.00 on it out of my allowance, so it wasn't like I'd taken money from my savings account or hit them up for extra cash. However, the mere fact that it showed an expensive jewelry purchase caught her attention, but thankfully, it didn't specify the type. But being that she somehow noticed Jasmine proudly wearing a new charm bracelet, she managed to put two and two together and asked if I'd given it to her, and I reluctantly said yes.

So, needless to say, she gave me a stern talking to about being involved with a much younger inexperienced girl, who I'd once viewed as a little sister. And just like my father, she told me to leave her alone. And she also warned me about what the consequences of touching her could lead to, highly emphasizing incarceration. But she didn't tell him, and that was a huge relief because we'd already had a conversation about Jasmine along those lines. And I'd ignored his warning and bought the bracelet after our talk. I was in love with her, and I couldn't stay away. Even though I was in college with numerous pretty girls throwing themselves at me, my heart belonged to a gorgeous, sexy girl in high school, and I was wholly devoted to her. And I was willing to risk everything, including my freedom to have her in my life.

We knew our parents were becoming increasingly concerned about our relationship and trying hard to squash it. She couldn't have sleepovers with my sister anymore when I was home from school, and Cathy had to always be between us at family gatherings. But no matter how hard they tried, they couldn't keep us apart. Because at the end of the day, they were fighting a losing battle! They just didn't know it! Because there were weekends that I'd make the two-hour drive home from college, and we'd spend the day together, and I'd drive back without them ever knowing that I was in town. Unbeknown to them, some weekends, I drove home both days.

Over the next few weeks, I found myself leaning hard on my best friend Pete, more and more. We'd gone to college together and maintained an extremely close relationship afterward. He's a much sought after divorce attorney and possesses a lot of wisdom for his young age. This guy is also a lot of fun to hang out with, and I can always depend on him when I need someone to lean on and set me straight.

He's not a Leah fan, nor is she a fan of his. He thinks she's too bitchy and demanding, and she thinks he always sides with me no matter what. But, that's not necessarily true because he's called me out on a lot of things dating back to college. I told him about Jasmine, and he sure as hell didn't approve and had no problem letting me know it. He called me a cradle robber and asked how I'd feel if Cathy was seeing an older guy? So, I told him that I'd be okay with it if I knew the guy's heart and intentions were pure like mine for Jasmine.

And he eventually understood that I was in love with her, and he did end up supporting me because he knew I wasn't some older, more experienced guy trying to take advantage of a young, innocent girl. He also knew I was committed to her, and she had my heart forever. I could've slept with a different girl every night, but I stayed faithful to Jasmine. Of course, I longed for sexual release, but I took care of that in other ways. In fact, I often refer to my right hand as Mr. Standby.

My parents had booked the country club, where we are members, to hold Cathy's party and spared no expense. They'd hired a highly sought after catering company and her favorite local band, and I purchased the gold bracelet that I knew she liked and had it engraved, with the inscription, best little sister ever.

But the week leading up to her surprise party, she asked me to come over because she'd received an unsigned birthday card with no return address postmarked from Japan. And we were both puzzled as to who it was from because neither one of us could think of who would have sent it. We didn't know anyone affiliated with Japan, yet I'd received a similar card from there when I turned twenty-five.

Her card read," There's no way I could let your milestone twenty-first birthday pass without at least acknowledging it. I wish you a lifetime of happiness and immeasurable fulfillment because if anyone deserves it, it's you."

"Julian, I don't want to upset you, but you have to be wondering the same thing as I am. Is it possible that this card is from Jasmine?"

"Yeah, you're right! That's exactly what I'm wondering because remember, I received a birthday card from there too with a very similar wording for my twenty-fifth birthday. Is it possible that they moved to Japan? If so, that would explain a lot. It would explain why I can't locate her in the states!"

"I don't know because I can't believe Mr. Daniel would move to a foreign country. He hated traveling outside the states on business, and somehow, I can't picture him watching sumo wrestling and attending tea ceremonies. He's more the football and basketball type, so I think we're grasping at straws because we want them to be from her. But it's probably a relative or a friend that travels there from time to time who enjoys making us wonder who the cards came from."

"Yeah, you're probably right. So, kiddo, how are things with Brian?"

"Well, things are good, and he should be coming over within the hour to take me to an early dinner. He's a good guy."

"Okay, well, so far, so good. I like Brian, but if you ever need me to straighten his ass out, just let me know, and I'll kick it real good for ya! I love you, little sister." Reaching out, I embraced her.

"Alright big brother, I love you too, and I'll certainly let you know if he steps out of line." Giggling gleefully, she broke our embrace.

I went home and looked for the card I'd received from Japan so that I could scrutinize it. It took me a minute to find it, but I eventually remembered where I'd put it. I knew what Cathy had said about wishful thinking, and even though I'd had the card for a while, it did faintly smell like a perfume that Jasmine used to wear. Or maybe, I was trying to make something be there that wasn't. Upon very close, precise examination, I couldn't find any clue as to who the card came from, and that was disappointing because I still didn't have any idea of her whereabouts.

When I was with Leah, I tried hard to be more engaged in planning our wedding, but as hard as I tried, I couldn't feel happy or content. I felt more like a drowning man looking for a lifeline, and I felt guilty for feeling that way because she deserved better than that. She didn't need a 215 PD albatross hanging around her neck, weighing her down.

And on the occasions that we had sex, it was no more than a physical act, my body responded to, but not my heart and mind because they felt somewhat numb! Jasmine had been out of my life for years now. Yet I thought about her every day, wondering where she was and who she was with. But recently, it never slacked up because I thought about her all the time. It was as though a switch had been triggered and refused to be dimmed or turned off. It was stuck on one channel, and I couldn't change it, no matter how desperately I tried! It was all about Jasmine!

Maybe it was because she would be turning twenty-one soon, and we were supposed to get married, or maybe, it was because my wedding day was drawing nearer, or perhaps it was a combination of the two. All I know is, I found myself overwhelmed and struggling with day to day activities. I'd always loved my job, but now quite often, I found it difficult to concentrate.

Chapter 3

The night of Cathy's party, she was surprised because we'd concealed it well. She thought we were simply having a family dinner at the country club to celebrate her birthday and included Brian, so when they walked in, and we all jumped out and yelled, happy birthday, you could see the happiness and sheer surprise etched across her face. She was beaming, and that made me feel good. Thankfully, it took my mind off Jasmine for a while.

But when she opened the gift that I'd bought for her, her eyes lit up, and she hugged me tightly. And that gesture reminded me of when I'd given Jasmine her charm bracelet and cleverly disguised engagement ring. Cathy had helped us to have a precious few moments alone, and Jasmine's eyes were sparkling like the stars in the night sky, and we kissed passionately. I also asked her to marry me when she turned twenty-one. Therefore, it was a special moment that I'll never forget because it is seared in my mind and heart forever.

So it didn't exactly help when my parents projected pictures on a wall of Cathy growing up through the years because there were pictures of Jasmine and me too, and my heart ached. And there was one picture in particular, where the three of us were at my High School graduation, and they were helping me hold up my diploma. I looked over at Cathy, and I could see the pain in her eyes too. She missed and longed to have her back in her life, just as I did. She'd left an enormous painful gaping hole in both of our hearts. And it felt as though mine was growing deeper and broader with each passing day.

The food was good, and the band was on point and played a wide variety of music. And for a few hours, I felt a measure of happiness as we did the electric slide and other group dances. But then, Leah wanted to slow dance, and I did so reluctantly.

And as we slowly danced to what she said was her favorite slow jam, she whispered into my ear seductively, " Julian, I want to be with you tonight. It's been a while, and I want you."

She was pressing up against me, but sex wasn't on my mind, so I didn't get an erection. Tonight, I wanted and desperately needed to be alone with my thoughts, but I was wondering how I could tell my fiance that without hurting her feelings?

"Hey, please don't take this the wrong way, but I'm a little tired after all this dancing, and I just wanna go home and crash. But you look amazing, and I'll make it up to you soon. I promise." Seeing the look of disappointment etched across her face made me feel bad, but I quite simply wasn't in the mood.

" Okay, I guess I'm a little tired too. Although, I've never known a man to turn down sex! And you will most definitely have to make this up to me!"

Quickly turning away from me, she walked away hastily, and Cathy came where I was.

"Hey, is everything okay?"

"Yeah, I think so. Leah's a little upset with me, but we'll be okay. So, please don't worry about me. I just want my little sister to enjoy the rest of her special night because turning twenty-one is a biggie, so embrace it fully.

 "Okay, Julian, but I'm here for you if you need to talk later."

"I appreciate that, but we can talk sometime tomorrow. Because right now, I'm going to find Leah, and we're going to cut out. Reaching out, we embraced, "I love you, Cathy."

"I love you too, and thanks again for the beautiful bracelet, and the inscription brought tears to my eyes. You're the best brother any girl could ever hope to have, and I want you to be happy, but sadly, I don't think you are."

I didn't respond to that; we broke our embrace, and I went to tell our parents goodnight. And then, I found Leah, who appeared slightly agitated, standing in a corner, although she tried hard to hide it when my parents walked over.

"Leah, Julian, said you guys are getting ready to leave, so Robert and I wanted to say goodnight and that it was nice to see you. Maybe, you all can come over to dinner next Sunday around three. You'll soon be a member of the family, and you need to become more accustomed to eating my cooking." Smiling, she reached out and gave her a quick hug.

Forcing a smile, she graciously accepted, "Yes, mam, it was nice to see you all too. It was an amazing party, and yes, we'd love to come to dinner. And I'm looking forward to it because everything I've eaten so far has been delicious. You're an excellent cook."

"Okay, well, thank you, Leah, and we're looking forward to seeing you guys next Sunday. Son, please drive safely, and I'll talk to you tomorrow."

Walking toward the car, we were virtually silent. Others were around, so Leah kept quiet. But as soon as we got in the car and exited the parking lot, she went off immediately.

"What in the hell is wrong with you lately? We haven't had sex in almost two months, and you seem to be perfectly okay with it. It's not like we make love all that often, but it was at least a couple of times a month! What's going on with you, Julian?! Something is eating away at you, and it's affecting us! I thought this relationship would be easy because we don't have kids and all that crazy outside drama to deal with! But we're still dealing with something, even though I have no idea what it is!"

"Are you seeing someone else? Is that what this is all about?" As she glared at me, her voice was very high pitched and accusatory. Folding her arms across her waist, she held her head back with her lips, pursed tightly together as though she was bracing herself for my answer.

"No, of course not."

When we made it to her townhouse, I didn't want to leave things as they were, so I got out and went in to talk. We took seats at the kitchen counter directly across from each other, and she fidgeted in her chair as she stared at me before saying anything.

"Do you resent me for seeing my ex-boyfriend a couple of times after we started dating?"

"No, I don't! I fully understood why you did that! You still had unresolved feelings for him, and you needed closure, and I wanted you to have it. I didn't want you to go through life with or without me wondering what if because it would've eaten away at you. Sometimes not knowing why has to be worse than knowing! Because if you have answers, at least, you don't have to wonder why."

Looking at me with a faint smile, she sighed, "Yeah, you're right because I did need that, and you were incredibly supportive and understanding at a time when I needed it the most. So, I guess I need to cut you a little slack. I know I can be incredibly selfish and self-absorbed at times, but I know what I want, and that's a life where I don't have to share my children's father. Because I want them to be the center of our world like I am my parents, and we can have that, but you need to meet me halfway. It's obvious that something has been bothering you for a while now, but you refuse to tell me what! Maybe I can help you!"

"No, I appreciate it, but I'm okay. I know I've been a little out of sorts lately, but things are going to get better. I'm going to address my demons and shortcomings and come to terms with them."

"Well, I sure hope so because my patience is growing thin!" Getting up slowly, she poured us a glass of red wine as we continued to talk about life in general. Because I think we were too afraid to look closely at our challenges. We both have baggage that desperately needs to be addressed and discarded, but for some reason, I couldn't find a way to let mine go. And there are moments; I feel as though she's still struggling too. Sometimes voices from the past speak to us whether we want to hear them or not. Also, memories can engage us and refuse to fade away, no matter how badly we need or want them to.

I went home, about an hour or so later, went to bed immediately, and I found myself thinking about the night that Jasmine had snuck into my bedroom, and we'd made love. It was as though I could feel her soft sensual hands all over my body, and it was responding to the mere thought of her touching and gently caressing my manhood. I could also taste her, so much so that I ended up giving myself sexual pleasure; it was intense and felt oh, so good. I also found myself moaning and softly calling her name, and although I wasn't necessarily proud of it, for a brief moment, I felt alive! And that was something that I hadn't felt in months.

The following day, I found myself struggling to get out of bed. Thank goodness it was Sunday, and I didn't have to go to work. So, I decided to make it a day of self-reflection. I'd been distracted lately, and it was gradually eating away at the fabric of my relationship with Leah.

We've had challenges along the way because of my unresolved feelings for Jasmine. She'd also had issues with her decision to break up with her ex-boyfriend, Thomas, of two years, simply because he had a kid from a previous relationship. She said she'd tried but could never get comfortable with it, although the child was born two years before their relationship.

I knew they'd shared something special, and I, of all people, understand that sometimes it's challenging to let go. Because I'd been trying to get Jasmine out of my system for years with very little success, so when she confessed that she'd seen her ex a couple of times after we initially started dating, I didn't have a problem with it at all. I didn't know if they'd slept together or not, but it wasn't an issue for me, so I didn't ask. Because if I had the opportunity to be with Jasmine again, I would do it without hesitation. Therefore, I would've been a hypocrite to hold that against her if she had.

Calling Cathy for a few minutes, I could hear in her voice that she was still excited about her party and gift, and that did my heart good because I love my kid sister. And she was the one person who missed Jasmine as much as I did. Our bond was extremely tight, and this was just one more thing that we shared.

That week flew by, and the next thing I knew, Leah and I were pulling up at my parents for Sunday dinner. Situations had been extremely tense between us for a couple of days after Cathy's party, but the tension had somewhat subsided. And I was trying hard to make things right between us. I was trying to be the man she needed me to be, and I wanted to be.

Entering my parents' home, I could smell turnips and fried chicken, so I was happy that my mom was preparing my favorite meal. Going into the kitchen where she was, I started looking around to see what else she was cooking and spotted my favorite side dish of golden-brown mac and cheese still bubbling, and my stomach started growling.

"Hey guys, come on in and make yourselves at home. Leah, you look nice, and I love that blue dress."

"Thank you, Mrs. Peterson, and you look nice too. Where is everybody? I saw Cathy and Brians' cars out front."

"They're on the patio with Robert and should be in any minute. He wanted to show Brian his new lounge chair, and he probably doesn't want to get out of it. I swear that man would sleep in that chair if he could. Giggling loudly, she put on an oven mitt, took cornbread out of the oven, and placed it on the stovetop.

Dinner is ready, and we can eat whenever they come back in, or Julian, you can let them know that we're waiting on them. And Leah, it would be great if you could help me put the food on the table because I've already set it.

"Sure, I'd be glad to."

I went to get everyone, and we sat down to an excellent dinner because my mom had undoubtedly outdone herself. I ate well after I was full because it was delicious, and I hadn't had a home-cooked meal in a few weeks. Although, my mom had taught me well how to cook for myself, and that was good because Leah wasn't big on cooking. She loved to go out to upscale restaurants and order take-out, but for me, that had gotten old. There's nothing like a good, piping hot, home-cooked meal.

"So, Leah, have you and Julian finalized most of your wedding plans? He said that you'd finally decided on a cake with the help of your mom."

"Yeah, Cathy, Julian was nice enough to let her help me decide. It's a beautiful, elegant cake, and your brother likes it too. It's six tiers and has tiny exquisite cupcakes on each side, and the flowers are going to be airbrushed and glazed with gold leaf. But everything else looks like frosted glass." Glancing my way, she smiled and took a sip of tea.

"Okay, Leah, that sounds like a cake you'd pick."

I could feel a little tension between them because Cathy is hugely protective and outspoken when it comes to me. She'd never tried to hide the fact that she didn't think Leah was the right woman for me, and she often referred to her as being too self-absorbed and pretentious. And there was some validity to that. So that puts her and Jasmine at opposite ends of the spectrum because Jasmine was spoiled rotten, but she always considered other people's feelings, whereas Leah pretty much thinks about her own.

We ate dinner and made small talk about a myriad of topics ranging from the latest movies to politics and sports to wedding plans.

"Well, Leah, Allison, and I are all set for the wedding rehearsal dinner at the country club because we've paid the deposit, so we're good. And the catering company is booked with the menu being everything that you requested to have. We were even able to find the flowers you want in Florida, and they'll be shipped here, the day before."

"Thank you, Mr. Peterson, because that time will be here before we know it. And Mrs. Peterson, dinner was delicious, but I ate way too much."

"Well, I'm glad you enjoyed it because Sunday dinners are a big deal in our family. There's nothing like breaking bread together."

"Oh yeah, that reminds me, my parents are planning to invite you all to a dinner party soon, so our families can get better acquainted. My mom says it's long overdue, and I completely agree. Our families will be united in a matter of months, and I'm excited about everyone getting to know each other better beforehand."

Alright, sweetie, we're looking forward to getting to know your family better as well. And Robert and I have really cut back on working Saturdays, but Fridays are good too, so just let us know.

"Yes, mam, I'll do that."

After a decadent mouth-watering German chocolate cake for dessert, I took Leah home.

When we got there, I knew she wanted to have sex when she said she was going to slip into something a little more comfortable because those were her code words for wanting sex. But thankfully, her mother called her, and I went home quickly because once again, I wasn't in the mood.

The following day, I decided to call Pete to see if he could meet me for lunch, and luckily he could. So we decided to go to Burger Palace because their food is good and their service is quick. They guarantee your food in fifteen minutes or less, or it's free, but I'd never hold them to that because everybody needs to get paid for their services.

Arriving at the restaurant, I spotted Pete waiting in his car. So I parked right next to him, and we exited simultaneously.

"Hey, bruh, what's up? Your voice sounded a little shaky over the phone, and you look a little on edge." Reaching out quickly, we fist-bumped.

"I'm okay. I just need to talk."

As soon as we entered the restaurant, a hostess greeted us promptly and led us to a table smiling, as we took our seats.

Alright, now tell me what's going on with you!"

I was getting ready to speak when a cheerful-looking waitress came to take our orders and went over the house specials at record speed. She spouted them off so quickly that she could've been an auctioneer and deserved an enormous tip just for that. And we both decided to order a medium-well jumbo bacon cheeseburger and beer-battered onion rings. I also wanted to order a beer to wash it down but thought better of it. I'm not much of a drinker, but occasionally, I do indulge in an ice-cold draft beer or two. However, today, I settled for raspberry tea.

Immediately after the waitress left our table, Pete looked at me intently and frowned, "Let's hear it, man, what's eating at you?"

Drawing my gaze to the tabletop, I felt uncomfortable, "Hey, I've been feeling slightly out of sorts lately, and I'm having a hard time pulling myself together. I've been struggling for a while now, and I don't know how to fix this. I'm feeling somewhat overwhelmed."

"Alright, is this work-related or personal?"

"It's personal, and to be honest, it's causing some major issues in my relationship with Leah."

Smiling cheerfully, the waitress came with our food and drinks in under ten minutes, so we cut off our conversation mid-sentence until she left.

"Alright, bruh, what were you saying?"

"Man, I don't know where to start because I don't understand what's going on with me. I'm getting married in a matter of months, but I'm not feeling happy like I should be. Instead, I'm feeling a little depressed and out of sorts."

"Okay, so are you trying to tell me that you're getting cold feet?"

"No, that's not it, or at least, I don't think it is."

"Well, bruh, I'm going to tell you exactly what I've told you before. If you're not sure about marrying Leah right now, then you should take a step back and think this thing through. There's nothing wrong with a postponement and making certain that it's what you want because it would be much better to have a broken engagement than end up in divorce court. Trust me when I say you don't want to travel that particular path. If you and Leah get married and have a kid or two and divorce, she's going to bleed your ass dry. And you'll be happy that your parents have such a big spacious house because you'll probably need to move back in, so you can continue to support Leah's extravagant lifestyle. So tell them to leave your old bedroom like it is, just in case!"

"I'm a divorce attorney, so believe me when I tell you that I've seen it happen time and time again. I've had numerous grown-ass men bawling like newborn babies on the other side of the table when I've helped their soon to be ex-wives wipe them out. It's not a pretty sight, and I don't want that to happen to you because you're my boy. So, I don't want to see your ass broke, picking up cans on the side of the road trying to hang on to your Benz, nor do I want to hear that you had to pawn your Rolex and sell your expensive designer suits, which I'd buy off of you myself if they weren't too big.

"And you already know that I'm not a big Leah fan because she's a little too self-centered for me, but she's not all bad. And I understand that she's an only child and spoiled rotten, so I try to cut her some slack. But, your girl is living a high society lifestyle, and she'll do anything to keep it. We're talking about someone who will drop $50.00 for lunch in a heartbeat while we try to stay under $20.00. And you're not going to like my next question, but I'm going to ask it anyway. Where does Jasmine factor into all this?"

"What do you mean?"

 "I mean, does this have anything to do with you trying to track her down?"

"I don't know, but maybe." Feeling somewhat uncomfortable by his question, I fidgeted in my seat because I knew Pete wasn't one to bite his tongue. He was going to tell me what I needed to hear, whether I liked it or not, and that's why I'd called him.

"Look, man, Jasmine has been gone for years now, and you have to find a way to make peace with the past and put it behind you because if you don't, it's going to destroy you eventually. I've seen you struggling with this for years now and watched every relationship you've had ended in complete disaster. I know she hurt you when she disappeared, but you have to find a way to let her and the heartache go."

"Yeah, well, that's a whole lot easier said than done! And believe me when I say I'm trying to move forward! I'm doing everything I can do to put her in the past, but it's not working. If anything, I think it's getting worse. But I'm doing everything I know to do!"

"Well, Julian, I hope you won't take this the wrong way, but that's not entirely true."

"What do you mean?"

"I mean, you're still looking for her." Leaning back in his seat, he took a sip of his tea."If you want to move forward, then you have to stop looking backward because, as harsh as this might sound, you can't go back in time. Sometimes, we have to make a clean break, and by that, I mean you need to stop looking for her because there's no magic button you can push to travel back in time and change things. It is what it is!"

Drawing my gaze to the tabletop, I just stared at it because I knew in my heart that he was right. I did need to stop looking for Jasmine for my own sake and sanity. It had been years now, and I had to find a way to let go and make peace with the past. But how could I do that when I had no idea why she'd never contacted me?

"Can you do that? Can you stop looking for Jasmine?"

Shrugging my shoulders, I looked up at him, "Maybe! I'm not sure, but I'm going to try."

"Okay, well, that's at least a start! You usually give me a flat out no, so you're making progress.

"Hey, that's enough about me. How are things with you and the new girl in your life?"

"Well, things are good. It's been four months, and we're taking things slowly. I like Megan a lot, so she has my undivided attention. This relationship is so different than the others I've had because I want to get to know her genuinely, so it's not about sex for me."

Chuckling, I stared at him," Alright, impostor, who are you, and what have you done with my boy?" Picking up a plastic knife, I made slashing motions toward him. "Don't make me cut you!"

Leaning back in his chair and laughing, he pointed at me, "Yeah, yeah, I know that's hard to believe because you know my track record, but it's true. I want more than casual sex! And trust me, when I say these words are foreign to me because back in the day, your boy was a hoe and a sex addict. But that addiction is over, and it's never coming back! Because I've come to my senses and been cured permanently, thankfully, without needing a shot of penicillin!." Chuckling, he took the last bite of his burger and motioned for the waitress to bring our check.

"Hey, bruh, I got you. I'm just happy that we could talk, and I'm going to get myself together and focus on the present and the future. Leah deserves a lot better than I've been giving her lately." Looking around, I spoke quietly, "Just between us; we haven't been intimate in a couple of months because the urge hasn't exactly been there when the opportunity has presented itself. But it comes strongly at other times.

Looking at me in sheer disbelief, he leaned forward in his seat. "Okay, so what's up with that?" Bruh, I hope you're not having a problem in that area because you're awfully young to need a little magic pill! Damn, you just turned twenty-six!"

"No, trust me, I don't need any help in that department at all! Your boy has plenty to work with, and he damn sure knows how to use it! So getting it up has never been a problem! It's just that I've been thinking about something that I shouldn't be, so I haven't exactly been in the mood lately when we're together, but I most definitely have strong urges. I just need to feel that way when I'm with Leah.

"Alright, but is it something or someone that's been on your mind? Because I get the feeling that it's the latter, and it all leads back to your time with little Ms. Jailbait. What in the hell did that girl do to you?"

Focusing entirely on me, he shook his head and leaned across the table, " Never mind answering that last part because I don't even want to know! But what I will say is that she must've put it on your ass like no other woman ever has! Bruh, she whipped you when she wasn't even old enough to vote! And I didn't say to have her driver's license because I hope like hell, she was at least sixteen when it happened!"

I didn't say anything, and the waitress came to pick up our check. And I was breathing a massive sigh of relief because I wanted to end our conversation. So I made small talk with her about the quick service for a moment, paid our check, tipped her generously, and we exited only to stand outside and talk for a few more minutes. But, he didn't mention Jasmine again, and I was glad. Because even though she was sixteen when we slept together, she'd been much younger when we started making out. But I couldn't expect anyone else to understand our connection and the love that we shared.

Leaving there, I called the florist and had a bouquet of pink roses sent to Leah's office. I chose pink because Jasmine is the only girl who I've ever bought red roses for. They're her favorite, and I didn't feel right buying them for anyone else. And I know that probably doesn't make sense to anyone other than me, but that's how I feel!

That evening, Leah called extremely excited about her bouquet and insisted that I come over. So, I showered and headed her way. And driving over to her townhouse, I couldn't help but feel slightly guilty because I knew that, in a way, I was cheating on my fiance'. And although it was emotionally and not physically, I was still harming our relationship, so I needed to stop.

Pulling up to her townhouse, I'd made up my mind that I was going to be a better man all the way around. Because Leah deserved so much more than I'd been giving her, she's a lovely, smart, intelligent woman, and any man would be happy to have her on his arm, and I wanted to be a man worthy of having her on mine.

Exiting the car slowly, I eventually made my way to the door. And as soon as I rang the doorbell, she answered, smiling."Hey, babe, thank you for the beautiful roses! You made my day." Closing the door quickly, she reached out to hug me, and that led to kissing, and I tried to show some passion, even though I wasn't quite feeling it.

"Okay, I feel like you're making an honest effort to make things right, and that means a lot to me. So, I'm hoping that you're going to spend the night here." Smiling at me seductively, she grabbed my hand as she led me to her bedroom.

"Julian, I've missed being with you, and I want you now." As we kissed and pressed up against each other, my body did slowly start to respond. I hadn't had sex in a while, and I needed that release because I refused to view self-gratification with my right hand as sex. Even though I did get off because Mr. Standby could be extremely useful in a pinch, and sometimes I found myself in one.

Slowly undressing each other, we laid on the bed, and she got on top of me, but not before I took precautions. I knew that she was on birth control, but I still refused to have sex without a condom until we said I do. So in that respect, our wedding night would be somewhat unique for us.

Chapter 4

Thoughts of my night with Jasmine tried hard to creep into my mind, but I fought like hell to keep them away because I could not or would not pretend like Leah was Jasmine. And eventually, I succeeded in banishing them as sexual desires took over, and I enjoyed the pleasure that only the warmth and softness of a female body could give me.

Afterward, she rolled over and put her head on my chest." Julian, this was our first step toward rebuilding our relationship, and it feels good. I want things to work out for us, and I think tonight is a turning point for us to move forward. Right now is our time to relish in pre-marital bliss as our wedding day fast approaches. It's a time for us to enjoy parties and make others jealous of what we share. We're a good looking, successful couple who can have it all!"

We got up, she cooked dinner, and I did feel slightly more engaged than I had recently, but the feelings I had for Jasmine were still somewhat distracting me.

Although, I was desperately trying to put the past in the past, where it belonged because no matter how badly I wanted to step back in time and hold her again, I couldn't. And I had to find a way to accept it and find peace within myself because that was something nobody else could do for me. It was something that I had to come to terms with on my own. And in my head, I knew that, but convincing my heart was an entirely different story.

The following morning, I got up and went home early to get ready for work. And when I arrived, my dad summoned me to his office before my computer had even booted up.

"Hey, son, come on in and take a seat." Entering and closing the door behind me, I took a seat directly across from his desk.

" So, what's up?"

"Well, I wanted to talk to you about something that your mom mentioned to me a few days ago."

"What did she say?" Feeling somewhat uneasy about that question, I tried to brace myself for what I was about to hear.

"Hey, don't look so serious! She just wanted to know if you guys would like a trip or cruise somewhere as a wedding present? You can go anywhere in the world because the price doesn't matter. We simply want y'all to enjoy yourselves."

Leaning forward in my seat, I was breathing a massive sigh of relief because I thought he was going to ask me if I was happy, and I didn't want to discuss that.

"Yeah, dad, a seven-day cruise would be an awesome gift, and I'm sure Leah would love it too."

"Okay, well, a cruise it is. Where would you two like to go? What do you think about Aruba? Do you remember what a good time we had when we went there with the Darrington's years ago? It's such a beautiful, peaceful place."

I felt my heart sink when he asked me that because it brought back a lot of fun but now somewhat painful memories. I'd just turned seventeen, and Jasmine and Cathy were twelve, and our poor parents worked overtime to keep up with us. Ironically, that was sorta the beginning of my forbidden relationship with her. We'd shared a kiss or two before the trip, but on this cruise, the three of us were watching a romantic movie under the night sky, and our parents had turned in because they felt confident that Cathy would be a buffer between us, and it did start that way.

She was between us everywhere we went on the ship, but she'd eaten something that didn't agree with her and went back to her room to lie down. However, we stayed to watch the movie. Jasmine laid her head on my shoulder, and we held hands because there was no one to stop us. And we also shared a few sweet kisses. That was a special night for us, and our poor unsuspecting parents never found out that we'd been left alone.

"Hey, son, what's wrong with you? You seemed a little spaced out for a minute. Are you sure you're okay?"

"Yeah, I'm fine. I was just thinking about how much fun that trip was, but no, I don't want to go back there."

"Okay, well, that was just a thought. Just tell me where, and we'll book it. "

"Well, I'd prefer to go somewhere we haven't gone on vacation with the Darrington's."

Looking at me a little funny, he leaned back in his chair and shook his head, "Julian, please tell me that you don't still have feelings for Jasmine Darrington because I thought that was just an infatuation that had long run its course. Am I wrong?"

Completely caught off guard, I couldn't answer because I didn't want to lie to him. And I knew the fact that we were one on one had left me cornered and exposed, and I felt too weighed down to try to deflect his question. It was like when he'd busted my ass about secretly seeing her years ago. I couldn't run, nor could I hide.

So, I quietly sat there, staring into space, longing for someone who I couldn't have.

"Okay, well, you don't have to worry about answering that question because I can see the answer in your face. Wow! You were actually in love with her, and I can tell by your expression that you still have deep, unresolved feelings that you're dealing with. Your relationship with her went a lot deeper than I, well, we all thought."

"Yeah, but that's all in the past, and I'm tired of looking back because it changes nothing. Jasmine isn't here, and I can't wave a magic wand and make her appear, nor can I press a magic button and go back in time to change things, no matter how badly I want to. I miss her." My voice was a little shaky, so I didn't say anything else.

"Well, I'll be damned! I knew something wasn't quite right with you, but I thought you were just second-guessing your relationship with Leah for other reasons because marriage is a huge step, but when you marry the right person, it's a beautiful thing. But it has to be the right one, or you're setting the stage for a total disaster."

"So, dad, how did you know that mom was the one for you?'

"As you know, your mother and I met in college, when I sorta accidentally, on purpose, bumped into her when she was trying out for cheerleaders. I'd noticed her for a

couple of weeks prior, and I thought she was the most
beautiful girl I'd ever seen, and I still feel that way. So I
spotted her heading to tryouts, and I timed it so that
we'd collide, and we've been inseparable ever since.
There's no other woman for me, so I guess I understand
how you feel about Jasmine. Why don't you try to find
her?"

"I've been looking for years! But it's like her entire family
has disappeared from the face of the earth. I went online
and found out that Mr. Daniel sold his company shortly
after they moved for an enormous fortune, but other
than that, there's no paper trail that I've been able to
find. I've run into one brick wall after another."

"Yeah, well, that's all I've been able to find out too. And
I'll never understand why Daniel or Carla haven't
reached out to us because we were inseparable for
years. Daniel Darrington is a brother to me, and Carla is
my sister. So I can't understand any of this either, but I
hope to someday."

"So what are you going to do? Are you sure that you
want to marry Leah?"

"Hey, don't get me wrong, I care deeply for her. I do,
and I'm going to be a good devoted husband. But
Jasmine will always have a special place in my heart,
and I'll always wonder what if! It's just something that I
have to live with, but I'll be okay. So, please book us a
cruise to Barbados."

"Okay, if you're sure? I'll book it."

"Yeah, I'm sure, and Leah will love it, but I'm going to let it be a surprise since I'm in charge of our honeymoon destination. I appreciate you and mom doing this for us. It's an awesome gift."

"Well, you're more than welcome."

When I made it back to my office, I felt sad because old feelings and memories had managed to infiltrate my mind, and I was struggling to banish them once and for all. I couldn't enjoy the present anymore because the past was overwhelming me, and I didn't know how to make it stop. So many fond memories were flooding my mind that they left me longing to step back in time, if only for a moment. I just needed to know why Jasmine never contacted me, and perhaps, I could get over it and be happy and fulfilled again.

The next couple of weeks flew by, and I found myself struggling more and more as Jasmines' twenty-first birthday loomed closer. And I was having a hard time holding myself and my relationship with Leah together.

She wanted and needed more from me than I could physically or emotionally give her during this time, but I tried. So instead of giving her the time and attention that she needed and deserved, I distracted her with fancy designer clothes and expensive jewelry, and she seemed okay with that.

And sadly, I found myself back on the internet, searching for Jasmine to no avail. So, in addition to not paying Leah any real attention, I had the guilt and shame of looking for another woman in my spare time, and even while I was at work. My life was spiraling out of control, and I had no idea how to fix it. Without being present, she was in my head and my heart, and I couldn't let her go. She had a hold on me, and I had to find a way to pry it loose or to, at the very least, lessen her iron grip!

And as much as Leah loved expensive jewelry and clothes that soon got old. Besides, she already had more clothes than she could probably ever wear. She was just like my mother and sister in that respect because they also had closets full of designer clothes from The House of Drayden. The owners and head designers were a husband and wife duo from Atlanta named David and Lauren Drayden, who my parents know relatively well as business contacts. And that was Jasmines' favorite clothing line too.

The next couple of months flew by, and my relationship with Leah limped along, and her parents invited mine to a dinner party like her mom said she would, and my parents graciously accepted.

And during that time, Leah got a standing job offer from New York, where she'd lived and worked for several years as a photojournalist for the New York's times. It was also where she'd dated her ex-boyfriend, Thomas, who also worked there as a high-powered well-known political columnist. And I genuinely believe that she would've married him if he didn't have a child from a previous relationship.

She'd turned the position down, but there were moments that I think she was second-guessing herself. In that respect, I think we were both struggling with unresolved feelings from our past, so could we build a solid foundation on that? Could a union between us survive haunting echoes from our previous lovers? Because the voices in my head were becoming louder!"

But despite our increasing, glaring red-flags, we still went full speed ahead with our wedding plans. Leah, with the help of her mom, chose a wedding gown and selected dresses for her bridesmaids. And I decided on my tux as well as the ones for my groomsmen.

We'd finalized the menu and chose the flowers, so everything was set for our six o'clock candlelight ceremony that was to take place on the rooftop of a revolving art gallery. Closing the roof would give the illusion of darkness so that countless candles would be the main lighting. It was a beautiful space, and our ceremony was being billed by many as the wedding of the year. Our families are of high profile because Leah's parents are good friends with the mayor of our city as well as the governor of the state. And my parents are well acquainted with them too. Therefore a lot of interest was being shown in our union, so our guest list had topped two hundred fifty people. But most of them were invited by Leahs' family because they're all about status and maintaining a spot in high society. So our wedding would be costly, but they could well afford it.

Things for me had somewhat mellowed out, but one night a week before Jasmines' twenty-first birthday, I found myself dreaming once again about the only time that we'd made love. She'd snuck into my bedroom, and it was supposed to be just to make out because I knew she was young and still a virgin, and I didn't want to pressure her in any way, shape, or form. I loved her deeply, and I was more than willing to wait until she was of age. But when she undressed and got in bed with me, things got out of hand quickly. Her body was incredibly soft, and she kept touching me ever so softly and timidly that it drove me crazy with desire. Not to mention the sweet perfume she had on was intoxicating.

We'd started just kissing, and she was trying hard to keep me quiet because we were at my parents' house, although my room was on the opposite end of the hall from theirs. But I was moaning with pleasure, so she kept telling me to quiet down. We gave each other oral sex, and that's where we should've left things, but our love and passion overtook us, and the next thing I knew, I was asking her if she was sure. And in that moment of unbridled passion, I made the conscious decision not to use a condom but to withdraw instead. I loved her, and I didn't want anything between us because I only wanted to feel her.

When I very gently penetrated her, I could feel that she was a virgin, and that was something that I'd never experienced before. She felt amazing, but I was as gentle as I could be. My thrusts were slow and controlled, but I soon found myself moaning with pleasure as the intensity grew, and I became lost in a sea of ecstasy and had waited too late to pull out because I'd started to orgasm. So I was telling her how much I loved her. And that I'd never meant to do it inside of her. But we'd get married if anything had happened, and I meant every word I said! If she'd gotten pregnant, I would've married her without hesitation, but that didn't happen! And I found myself waking up from a wet dream and had to get up to change my bedding and shower.

Over the next few days, my thoughts were focused and consumed with memories of Jasmine, and I felt more out of sorts than ever before. At this point, I think I was suffering from a mild case of depression and anxiety. Her birthday was fast approaching, and I was utterly overwhelmed with thoughts that refused to be overlooked or ignored. So, I found myself trying to find a way to deal with her milestone birthday, and alcohol was at the top of my list. I bought myself a bottle of rum and a six-pack of cokes to ease my pain. I figured if I got hammered enough, it would pass by quickly, and I wouldn't have to deal with my emotions because they'd be numb. Therefore, I'd feel nothing. And nothing was what I desperately wanted and needed to experience.

Her birthday fell on a Saturday, and I was happy because I didn't have to go to work. So, I called Cathy to see if she was home, and she said she'd be there all day. I told her that I'd see her later but immediately headed that way.

When I got there, I let myself in and turned off the alarm quickly, and Cathy came where I was in the family room.

"Hey, Julian, I'm surprised to see you so soon. When you said later, I had no idea that you meant ten minutes later." Giggling loudly, she pulled her hair up in a high ponytail.

"Yeah, well, I know that mom and dad are out of town, so I decided to drop by and check on my kid sister." Winking, I headed past her to the kitchen for something to eat, and she was hot on my trail."

Cool, but your sister is twenty-one now and entirely capable of staying at home alone because I have for years. Besides, this place is probably more secure than Fort Knox. So try again! Why are you here so early? And mom made several individual breakfast casseroles that I can pop in the microwave. So why don't you take a seat, and I'll heat up a couple, and we also have fresh cut-up fruit, and that strawberry tea that you love.

As soon as I took a seat, she started preparing breakfast for us. "So once again, Julian, why are you up and over here so early on a Saturday morning?"

Shrugging my shoulders, I looked at her, "Okay, maybe, I just want to talk to you." The microwave went off, and she fixed me a plate of casserole and a bowl of fresh cantaloupe, watermelon, and honeydew melons along with a glass of tea. "Hey, thanks, I'm starving."

Grabbing her plate, she sat down right across from me. "Okay, so where's Leah?"

"Well, I suppose she's at home, but I haven't talked to her this morning, and she has plans with friends later. Come on, Cathy, and cut me some slack, please!" I took a bite of casserole, and it was excellent.

"Alright, I'm sorry because I know that today is Jasmines' birthday, and I'm missing her too. So, I'm pretty sure that's what this is all about. But Jasmine has been gone for years now, and you've always been sad, but I can look at you and know that somehow this year is different. Is it because she's twenty-one today, or is it because your wedding day is only a few months away? And once you say I do to Leah, you'll have to stop dreaming about reconciling with Jasmine!" Picking up her glass, she took a sip of tea, but she never stopped looking at me.

"Well, you most definitely hit the nail on the head because I'm missing her like crazy today. Your psychology courses are paying off. I guess I just need to understand why she has never called or contacted me, and I'd be okay. She walked out of my life and disappeared into thin air, and she's never contacted me. So, I guess I'm hurt and confused because I thought she loved me. But maybe, I was wrong!"

"Hey, although I can't tell you why she hasn't contacted you, there's one thing that I can tell you without hesitation and beyond any shadow of a doubt. She loved you, and she didn't care who knew it."

"Do you remember how she would flirt with you when she was only five, and you were ten?
She'd prance around, making goo-goo eyes at you, with her hands on her hips doing everything she could to get your attention. She'd even put on her mom's high heels and try to walk in them to impress you."

"Yeah, of course, I remember. It was hilarious watching Jasmine batting her eyes at me or trying to hold my hand, stumbling around in heels. I couldn't turn for that little girl." My voice was shaky because I felt incredibly emotional.

"Yeah, and as we got older and girls came to see you, she'd try to stake her claim. Do you remember when she was only ten and told Cory, your first date, that she was just a mere bump in the road when she came over? And she did everything; she could think of to annoy her, like sneezing and clearing her throat constantly, until her parents made her leave the two of you alone to watch a movie. Then she offered to take you guys something to drink and put salt in poor unsuspecting Cory's tea!" Laughing hysterically, as she recalled the event, she reached out to high-five me.

I couldn't help but laugh too, "Yeah, of course, I remember that! I also remember her telling my prom date, Amanda, that she was around me all the time, strongly suggesting that we had something going on. And the only reason I wasn't taking her was that she was too young to go, so I had to reluctantly settle for her but not to feel bad about being my second choice by default. She'd turned twelve, and I'd be lying if I said I hadn't started to see her differently because I no longer saw her as my little sister. I saw her as a beautiful girl, who I found myself undeniably attracted to. Quite honestly, I think I've always liked her, even when we were little kids. Jasmine is beyond special. She's the type of girl that comes into a man's life, and you never forget her."

"Hey, I knew you cared about her, but I don't think I knew how much until just now. You were deeply in love with her." Pausing momentarily, she looked me straight in the eyes, " So, I have to ask if that's in the past tense?" Her focus was squarely on me, so I drew my gaze out the window and saw a hummingbird fly by.

For a moment, I sat there in complete silence as I struggled to find the words to answer her, "Hey, just between you and me, I don't think I'll ever stop loving her, but I have to move on as she has. I long to go back in time, but I can't." I could feel tears well up in my eyes as I held them closed for a brief moment because I refused to shed them in front of my little sister.

"Come on, Julian, how can you possibly marry Leah feeling like you do about Jasmine? You won't be happy and neither will she! Besides, she has to know that you're not all that thrilled about your upcoming wedding. It's been obvious to me since you made your announcement, and mom and dad have mentioned it too. So surely, Leah has to know that something isn't quite right. She's all about status and her image, but she's either fooling herself or conveniently blind when it comes to your engagement. Anybody who knows you can tell that you're not actually in love with her!"

"Cathy, please don't get me wrong, I care deeply for Leah, and I'll be a good husband and provider. And in a way, I do love her. It's just not in the same way that I love Jasmine, but that's never going to happen with anyone. But I care enough to treat her well, and you know that I'm not the type to step out, so I'll be completely faithful."

"Yeah, big brother, but you can only pretend for so long. I care about the postman, but I don't want to marry him. Leah is a lot of things, but she's not stupid. She has to know that she doesn't have your whole heart. Let's just say that you get married, and she gets pregnant, and all of a sudden, you realize that you can't pretend to be happy or content anymore, then what?"

"Deep down, she has to know that this is all wrong, but right now, she's so excited and caught up in the fantasy of a beautiful elaborate wedding with the perfect gown and venue that she doesn't see you. I'm sorry, but you never should've proposed to her! Because that beautiful ring doesn't belong on her finger!"

"Well, actually, I didn't. Leah, more or less, said, let's get married, and I just didn't say no and bought her the ring that she picked out. And besides, I have to find a way to put Jasmine in the past. I need to forget about her like she's forgotten me!"

"But today can't be that day because it's her twenty-first birthday, and it was supposed to be our wedding day."

With her mouth hanging open, she stared at me, "What? What did you say?"

"One night, when she was only sixteen, we made a vow to get married on this day, and I meant that. When I gave her that charm bracelet for her sweet sixteen, one of the charms was an engagement ring that only the two of us knew about. We wanted to tell you, but we didn't want to involve you in it in case anyone found out. I hope you can understand that."

Shaking her head affirmatively, " Yeah, I understand, but it's still a shock because I had absolutely no idea about this. So I'm wondering what else I don't know! "

"Alright, well, now you understand why today is so hard for me. And I'm going to throw myself a pity party later, but tomorrow, I'll be fine. Besides, I have to be because I'm getting married in a few months."

"But today, I can't help but wonder what she's doing and if she's thinking about me. I just want to know that she's happy and doing well. And I desperately need to know why she never got in touch with me, and maybe I could be okay and move forward. It's wondering why that's killing me! I miss her so much!"

Reaching across the bar, she caught my hand. "Come on, Julian; I hate to see you like this. I knew you two had grown extremely close, but I had no idea that you'd proposed to her. As I said, this is a shock!"

"I remember having to cover for you guys while you all snuck around and stole kisses. But in the very beginning, I used to ball you out about leading her on, but I soon realized that you cared about her too. And our parents were always checking on you all or making me sit between you two. And you know how Jasmine was about taking chances. She was relentless when it came to you. I can hear and see her now, whispering, okay, Cathy, you have to help us out. We just want to spend a little time together, and that's it. It's just kissing, so what's wrong with that? And she'd look at me with her piercing dark eyes in such a way that I'd have to say yes. " Letting my hand go, she took a sip of tea.

"Yeah, she could just look at me and smile, and my heart would melt. I'd do anything for her."

"Well, as I said earlier, I knew that you cared, but I didn't know how deeply. So, what are you doing later? Since you don't have plans with Leah, maybe we can just ride this day out together and reminisce. Brian is working today and hanging out with his brother later, so I'm free."

No, I don't have plans with Leah, but I wasn't kidding when I said that I was going to throw myself a pity party. I just want to be alone with my thoughts and do some self-reflection. So, I'll probably order takeout and have a few drinks. Who knows, maybe some alone time and a good nights' sleep will do me a world of good. Tonight was supposed to be our wedding night, and if I can't spend it with her, then I'd rather spend it alone." My voice was shaky once again, and I felt lost.

"Come on, Julian, I hate to see you so sad. Maybe you should concentrate on finding her. I know you don't want to hurt Leah, and although I don't necessarily like her ways. I do care about her feelings, and I don't want her to get hurt. I know it won't be intentional, but you will end up hurting her one way or the other. Just promise me that you'll think about what I've said."

"I promise, and I'm getting ready to go home. But I think I'll go on and order my food and pick it up on the way."

"Well, if you don't have anything particular in mind that you want to eat, mom made some delicious seafood gumbo and homemade dinner rolls. And she even baked a blueberry pound cake if you're interested.

"Of course, I am. Mom's gumbo is the best I've ever had."

"Okay, well, I'll fix you a plate. There's also ham and potato salad, so I'll fix you some of that too."

"Yeah! That would be great."

Pulling various containers from the refrigerator, she fixed me enough food for a small army.

"Thank you, little sister, but you must think I have people at home who I also have to feed ." Chuckling loudly, I reached for the bag, but she placed it on the countertop and reached out to hug me."

"Julian, I hope that you'll find the answers that only Jasmine can give you. But if not, I pray that you'll somehow be able to put this behind you and find peace and happiness. I love you."

"Yeah, and I love you too. And thank you, little sister, for always being here for me. It's like the inscription on your bracelet says; you're the best little sister ever. And I don't know what I would do if I didn't have you to talk to."

Picking up the bag from the countertop, I headed toward the door, and Cathy was close behind me. "Alright, Julian, please don't overindulge drinking because I've never known you to drink anything more than an occasional beer or two."

"Hey, don't worry about me! It's just a couple of drinks!" Winking at her, I opened the door and left.

"Returning home, I put my bag in the refrigerator and got online once again to search for Jasmine Danielle' Darrington, and countless names came up. So I narrowed the search to her age bracket, and that cut down on the list tremendously. But unfortunately, I still couldn't find her. It was as if she didn't exist anymore.

So, I heated my gumbo and killed time overeating and watching t.v., as I felt sorrier and sorrier for myself. I was wallowing knee-deep in self-pity as I thought more and more about Jasmine.

My buzzing phone startled me, and it was Leah.

"Hey, what's up?"

"Sweetie, I've sent you several texts and even called a couple of times, but I wasn't able to reach you. So, I was getting worried and thinking about heading your way because I can go out with my girlfriends another time? Are you okay?"

"Yeah, I'm fine. Please go out with your friends and have a good time. Besides, I'm tired, and I'm going to turn in early."

"Okay, but you haven't been yourself for a while because it seems as though something is constantly on your mind, and I hope it's me."

I didn't want to lie to her, so I remained silent.

"Come on, Julian, what's going on with you? Leading up to our wedding day is supposed to be a happy time for us, but I'm not blind, so I know that something isn't quite right. My parents have even asked me what's wrong with you?"

"Things will be better tomorrow, and we can move forward with our plans. I'm sorry that I've been so distracted lately, and I promise I'll do better. I just need a good night's sleep, and tomorrow will be a pivotal turning point in our lives. You'll see!"

"Okay, I sure hope so, and my friend Amy is here, so I'll see you tomorrow."

"Alright, well, enjoy, but don't party too hard." Faking a chuckle, I tried hard to sound upbeat, but on the inside, I felt like a drowning man.

Immediately after I got off the phone, I worked extremely hard to bury my sorrows with rum and coke, and pretty soon, I stopped adding the coke, and that was a huge mistake. Because I was so wasted that all I can remember was holding on to the handrails as I staggered upstairs to my bedroom and fell back on the bed to sleep it off. And I found myself somewhere between consciousness and unconsciousness, as I laid there looking up at the ceiling consumed with thoughts and emotions that alcohol seemed to have intensified. I was drunk, but not quite drunk enough to numb my mind or emotions.

I felt as though I was in the twilight zone as I laid there trying to imagine what our wedding night would've been like and what lingerie Jasmine would've worn. Would her lingerie have stayed on five minutes, or would I have removed it immediately? When out of nowhere, she suddenly appeared wearing a sheer red gown and got on top of me, kissing me passionately like we used to kiss all those years ago, whenever we could find time alone, and I was moaning with pleasure, " Jasmine, where've you been? Why didn't you call me?" I was holding her as tightly as I could and pressing up against her moaning. "I've missed you."

"Who did you call me?"

I was barely conscious, but I realized that although I was
seeing and kissing Jasmine, I was hearing Leah's
outraged voice coming from somewhere in the room, so
we weren't alone! Jasmine jumped up off me and left me
on the bed, but I didn't want her to disappear again and
reached out for her arm, only for her to yank it away.
"Jasmine, please don't leave me!"

"Who in the hell is Jasmine?'

I could hear Leah, and I knew what she was asking, but
I couldn't answer! I was highly intoxicated, but in a brief
moment of clarity, I knew the damage the name had
done. Because now I realized, even in my drunken state
of mind, that it wasn't Jasmine, who I'd been kissing!
She was only a figment of my imagination and had
never been here. It had been Leah! I'd just called my
fiance' by another woman's name!"

 As she was shaking me violently, she was also
screaming, "Wake the hell up, and tell me who Jasmine
is! Wake up!"

Lying across the bed, I was struggling within myself to
wake up and say something, if only to apologize, but I
couldn't because everything in my life went black.

Chapter 5

Eventually, coming to the following morning, I felt like my head was about to explode. It was pounding like someone was on the inside, wearing cleats and stomping my brain continuously. I also felt sick on the stomach, so much so that I had to run to the bathroom to be sick, and I barely made it in time. And that did make me feel somewhat better, so I took a quick shower, brushed my teeth, and took something for my excruciating headache.

I didn't remember a whole lot about last night, but I did vaguely remember calling Leah, Jasmine, or did that happen? Maybe, I was just so drunk that my mind had been playing tricks on me. Was it possible that I'd been hallucinating? I also knew that the only way I could know for sure would be to talk to Leah. But was I in a state of mind to make that call?

However, when I went downstairs to the great room, I knew it was all too real because the red gown that Leah had been wearing was on the floor, along with a picture of us torn into tiny pieces. So no, it hadn't been my imagination! I'd called Leah, Jasmine, at the worst time possible. I didn't have to wonder if she was devastated because I knew she was. We'd been passionately kissing when I called out another woman's name. Was that an unforgivable transgression? Could she forgive me for causing her such grief?"

My life was spiraling completely out of control, and I had to find a way to get it back on track and make things right with Leah. Or maybe, I needed to simply walk out of her life and let her find a man who could freely and completely give her his whole heart. Because no matter how hard I tried, I couldn't give her mine, and that wasn't fair.

Picking up my cell phone to call her, I thought better of it immediately. So, I decided to call Pete instead and asked him to come over.

"Alright, bruh, hang tight, and I'm on my way because you sound like hell. I sure hope you don't look or feel as bad as you sound."

As I waited for him to arrive, a million thoughts ran through my mind while I tried to come to terms with what I'd done. And I didn't feel good about myself. I'd hurt

someone, who I care about in a cruel but unintentional
way, and I had to try to make it right.

Within thirty minutes, Pete was ringing my doorbell, and
I answered it quickly.

"Damn, boy, what in the hell happened to you? Because
not only do you sound like hell, you look like it too!
Were you hit by a bus, a train, or both?"

"Man, come on in and take a seat." Closing the door
quickly behind him, he immediately went and plopped
down on the sofa.

"Alright, bruh, what's this all about? Come on and tell
me what's going on with you!" Concern clearly showed
in his face, and I knew he was worried about me.

Shaking my head and briefly closing my eyes, I took a
deep breath, "Hey man, what do you think is the worst
thing you can say to a woman when you're intimate?"

"Oh, hell, no! Please tell me you didn't call Leah by
somebody else's' name!! Please tell me you didn't call
her Jasmine!"

Drawing my gaze to the floor quickly in shame, I cleared
my throat, "Yeah, regrettably, I did."

Standing up abruptly, he stared at me, "How in the hell
did that happen?"

" It happened because I was sloppy drunk!"

"Who? You?"

"Yeah, me! I was having a rough time yesterday because it was Jasmine's twenty-first birthday, and I was missing her terribly and feeling sorry for myself. So, I tried to bury my sorrows, with an enormous amount of rum, and you know, I rarely drink hard liquor."

"Yeah, well, I know that hit your ass like a ton of bricks! And, I'm surprised that you could somehow get it up because too much rum ain't no joke, and it can paralyze that particular part of a man's body! Sadly, it can remain unresponsive for hours, refusing to salute for a sexy naked girl in bed with you, no matter how beautiful and fine she is. But then, that's another story."

"Well, I'm not sure if I could've, but it never went that far. I was lying across the bed, semi-conscious at best, when I saw who I thought was Jasmine, wearing a sheer red gown, and she got on top of me, kissing me passionately. And I think I asked, Jasmine, where've you been or something like that?" I picked Leah's gown up off the floor and threw it on the coffee table.

"I was drunk out of my mind, but I do vaguely remember hearing Leah's irate voice asking, who's Jasmine? She was also shaking me hard, trying to wake me up, but I must've passed out, and when I woke up, it was morning."

"Man, I've fucked up big time!"

Nodding his head, affirmatively, "Yeah, bruh, you have!" What in the hell are you going to say to Leah?"

"I don't know, so I was hoping you can tell me how I should handle this. I'd picked up the phone to call her earlier, but I chickened out and called you instead. What in the hell can I do or say to make this right?"

"Hey, I've never had to navigate these particular waters, but I do know that the longer you wait, the worse it's going to be. So if I were you, I'd face her today. I'd call and ask if I could come over, and I'd tell her about my past with Jasmine. And you need to emphasize that she walked out of your life years ago, and you haven't heard from her since. So she won't view her as a viable threat."

"But before you do that, you need to make sure that you want to go through with this wedding. Man, I'm the only one you told about young, beautiful, jailbait Jasmine in college. And in the beginning, I thought you were fucking crazy because you refused to date or sleep with anyone else after you committed to her, and I was astonished, to say the least. Because you could've spread more legs on campus than a gynecologist, but you chose not to. So that alone showed me how much you loved her.

"What young college boy in his right friggin mind turns down a buffet of perfectly good sex with no strings attached? And you, bruh, had a lot of girls wanting a piece of you. You're a tall, good looking, light skin brother with wavy hair and greenish-brown eyes. So girls were damn near throwing themselves at your feet, begging you to hit it, but miraculously to me, you turned them down time and time again. Some girl even pulled off her funky black panties at a party and threw them at you, and you stepped over them and walked away."

And although I'm a one woman's man now, and always plan to be, I was a straight-up hoe in college. I sowed so many wild oats that I almost choked. And, I'm not exactly proud of it, but I pretty much humped any girl who'd open her legs wide, hold still, and let me. But between us, I've never screwed an ugly girl, although now, looking back, maybe I should've hit one or two from behind, just for the hell of it, since I didn't have to look them in the face.!" Hysterically laughing when he said that, I laughed too. And that was something that I needed to do at that moment.

"Julian, you're a good guy, and I know you want to do the right thing, and you've certainly taught me something about love and devotion because I saw first - hand how devoted you were to Jasmine at such a young age. Even though I thought your ass was mentally unstable for turning down sex, sex, and more sex!"

"And although it took me a while to understand that there's a huge difference between love and lust, I finally figured out that I prefer love."

"Yeah, well, I figured that out a long time ago, when I was much younger, and I wanted to be with Jasmine. And no other woman has ever come close to making me feel like she does, but she's not here. And I have to face the fact that for whatever reason, she's not coming back. She made her choice, and she didn't choose me! So, I have to let her go!"

"Man, I've heard you say that time and time again over the years, and you still haven't been able to get her out of your system. What makes you think that this time will be any different?"

"Yeah, well, this time has to be different because I can't keep putting myself through this same crap. So, I have to find a way to get over her and let the dream of reconciling go. I have to do this for my own sake and sanity. It's been years, so why am I still struggling to free my heart?"

Abruptly, he put his hand on my shoulder, "Okay, bruh, you have to find a way to cut her loose, or if not, you need to cut Leah loose. She's bossy and self-centered as hell, but I'm sure she has some good qualities because I know you do care about her. So, if you're going to get married, you have to dig deep inside yourself and let Jasmine go. And I know it won't be easy because she's your first love and all, but you have to do it.

"So if I were you, I'd call Leah and ask if I could come over to talk. And if she says yes, apologize and tell her about Jasmine, but don't give her more info than she needs to know. Remember that this is strictly on a need to know basis. And do not under any circumstances tell her how young Jasmine was because that's none of her damn business! As a matter of fact, that's nobody's business! And the good thing about that is, there's no proof whatsoever."

Because whereas I know that you love her and weren't taking advantage of her, others might not see it quite that way. Some might see a grown-ass man, who was fooling around with a young, inexperienced girl, and society doesn't like that and has strong laws in place against it. And as I'm sure you're aware, some men have done prison time for such behavior! So whatever you decide to tell her, please don't mention Jasmine's age!"

"Yeah, okay, I hadn't thought about it like that, so thanks. Is there anything else that you can think of?"

"Hesitating, he stared at me for a brief moment, "Man, I just want you to be sure that you want to marry Leah.

Because it's like I keep telling you, it's better to have a broken engagement than an empty bank account. I know Leah has plenty of money, but I'm sure she'll want yours too. So please think about that, and I'm going to leave so that you can call her."

"No, just hang tight for a moment, and I'll call now. Besides, Leah probably won't agree to see me anyway, and I can't say that I could blame her if she said no. I'd be pissed off if a woman called me by another man's name, especially if we were in bed. That would sting like hell!"

"Yeah, bruh, that's a tough one! Although it would've been much worse if you'd been in the act of banging her. But I think if you sincerely pour your heart out and show vulnerability, without making excuses, I think she'll forgive you."

"Alright, well, I'm going to call her." I picked up my phone and hesitated for a moment before dialing her number. The phone kept ringing, and I was about to hang up when she finally answered.

"Hey, Leah, I would imagine that I'm the last person you want to hear from or talk to, but I want to see you. I'm sorry about last night, and I want and need to explain it to you."

"So, Julian, what is it that you're sorry about exactly? Are you sorry that you got drunk? Are you sorry that you had to be drunk to feel passionately for me? Or are you sorry that you called me by another woman's name?! Which is it, or are you sorry for all three?" Hearing her screaming at the top of her lungs so loudly, I knew Pete had undoubtedly heard every word!

"Leah, please, give me a chance to explain myself, and we can go from there. May I please come over?"

There was complete silence on the other end of the phone for a moment, "Okay, you can come!" Her tone was harsh and cold, and I understood that.

"Okay, I'm on my way."

Hanging up, I turned quickly to Pete, "Man, she's pissed, and I don't blame her because I've caused her a whole lot of pain."

"Yeah, I heard, but if you handle it right, I still think she'll come around if you're sincere and pour your heart out. Good luck, bruh."

"Alright, and I appreciate your coming over. You've helped me through some tough times."

Winking at me, he reached for the doorknob " Bruh, that's what friends are for, and you've always had my back too. I'll walk out with you."

Chapter 6

Driving over, I was racking my brain, trying to find the right words to say, but nothing I thought about seemed right. There were no magic words that could fix this, so I decided to speak from my heart. Otherwise, my apology would come off as scripted and insincere, and I didn't need to come off like that because I was genuinely sorry.

Pulling up, I sat in the car for a few minutes and stared at her townhouse. Then, I finally built up the courage to get out and ring her doorbell. Answering quickly, she moved aside for me to enter and slammed the door immediately behind me, causing pictures to shake on the walls.

Turning to face her, I could see the hurt and disappointment in her eyes, and I felt terrible that I'd caused her such pain, "Hey, Leah, I'm glad that you agreed to see me because I wasn't sure if you would."

Suddenly, she put her hands on her hips, "Well, that makes two of us because I wasn't sure either. But I decided that I should at least hear you out. So, tell me about Jasmine!" Her voice was forceful and demanding as she glared at me. "Let's take a seat."

"Okay," Following her, we took a seat at the dining room table, but I felt like I needed to stand back up.

"Alright, tell me who Jasmine is."

Quickly, I drew my gaze to the floor, "Well, she's someone, who I was very much in love with, and I felt at some point, we would've gotten married. But I haven't seen or spoken to her in about five years, and she's not a threat to us. She was best friends with Cathy, and she mentioned her yesterday. And I can't lie! I started wondering why she walked out of my life and never looked back because I know she did love me at one point. We were deeply in love, but that's in the past."

"Remember, when we first started dating, and you still had residual feelings for your ex-boyfriend Thomas?"

"Yeah, of course, I remember that, but we'd just broken up several months earlier! It hadn't been for years! And besides, we'd just started dating, but now, we're engaged, so you can't equate the two because one outweighs the other by far. I have a ring on my finger in case you've forgotten! So don't you dare attempt to compare the two!" Screaming, she held up her ring finger, pointed at it, and all but forced it in my face.

"Yeah, that's true. But the point I'm trying to make is this; I encouraged you to find closure with Thomas one way or the other because I, of all people, know how it feels not to have it. And you felt so much better after you had the opportunity to spend time with him and talk things through. And I also know that you were deeply in love with him, and if he didn't have a child from a previous relationship, you'd probably be married to him right now."

"Okay, you're right, I was in love with him, but I've never wanted to be with a man who has a child. But I made an exception for him, and maybe, I was selfish to let that come between us. But I didn't want to be second best to his kid, and I didn't want any drama from his child's mother. And isn't it ironic that I have to share you with a memory?"

"On paper, we're so perfect for each other. You're a tall, incredibly handsome, successful man with no kids. And I know this might sound shallow, but I'm a beautiful, desirable, successful woman with no kids. So, I've been wondering why this relationship is so damn difficult. We have financial security and very similar backgrounds, yet we're constantly struggling. And now I know, it's all because you're still trying to figure out why your ex-girlfriend left you years ago."

"But you have to choose whether you want a woman who's here in the flesh, and you can reach out and touch anytime you choose, or one who's just a memory because I won't knowingly be second best, especially to a memory. And as you know, I have a standing job offer in New York, so I need to know right now if I should take it." Pounding her fist forcefully on the table, she knocked off a glass coaster, but it didn't appear to break.

"Leah, I don't want you to go."

"Well, you sure as hell don't act like a man who wants me to stay! I also need to ask you another question, and I want you to be honest with me, even if it hurts."

"Okay." Looking at her, I could see that she was fighting back the tears, and that hurt because I was causing her that heartache and pain.

"If Jasmine showed up on your doorstep right now, would you still want me to stay?."

I couldn't answer such a hypothetical question, so I answered it with a question.

"Do you regret breaking it off with Thomas?"

"Okay, Julian, so where do we go from here?"

"Jasmine is not a part of my life anymore, and I accept that. I just need your forgiveness."

Suddenly, she stood up, "Our wedding is right around the corner, and I don't want to end up looking like a damn fool by you breaking our engagement! And I need more from you than what you've given me so far. Because I want and need more than an occasional roll in the hay when it feels like you're sleeping with me out of some kind of obligation, it feels good, but it lacks any real passion. Because when we make love, I want to know without a shadow of a doubt that you want me and only me."

"And I know your sister thinks that I'm a selfish, self-centered, spoiled little bitch, but I know what I want, and it's that simple. I want a husband who will love me and dote on me and our kids without any outside drama from an ex with kids. And now, you're bringing up some craziness from years ago that you need to let it go!"

"My parents are having a dinner party, so they can get to know you and your parents better, and I expect you to at least pretend to be happy until you resolve this, Jasmine nonsense. She left you years ago because she doesn't want to be with you, but I do. So, accept the fact that she never really loved you, and she's not coming back."

"I'll make you happy, but you have to let go of the past as I have. And then, we can get married and start a family of our own. So, it's time to stop pining away about what you thought you had with her and appreciate what you have with me. She was your past, but I'm your present and future, and I do love and want to be with you. So, I forgive you, but this better not happen again ever because I won't tolerate you having a physical or emotional affair with anyone!'

Reaching out, she hugged me, "I know it has to be frustrating not having the answer that only she can give you, but sometimes not getting an answer is your answer. She doesn't want to be with you, and you have to find a way to be okay with that. For heaven's sake, that was years ago! So let's put this behind us and move forward!"

Suddenly breaking our embrace, she ran her hands through her hair, "Please tell me that you haven't told your parents or sister about this because I couldn't face them if you have!"

"No, I haven't."

"Well, don't, and we're never going to discuss Jasmine again. As far as I'm concerned, she doesn't exist because I'm not going to let some woman who's just a memory end our engagement! We're going to get married just as we planned." Defensively folding her arms, she stared at me.

Her voice was a little high-pitched and filled with emotion, but at least she had forgiven me, and that was all that I could ask for.

"Okay, thank you for forgiving me, and I promise to do better. Would you like to go out to dinner later?"

"No, not tonight. And right now, I want to be left alone, but we can talk tomorrow."

Instinctively, I wanted to reach out and hug her, but her demeanor and stoic expression told me not to. She was still visibly upset and rightfully so, and I certainly understood how sometimes you need to be alone with your thoughts to self reflect.

"Alright, well, I'll call you in the morning."

As soon as I got home, I called Pete immediately and told him what had transpired. I also told him never to let on that he knew what happened. I felt slightly guilty for not confessing to Leah that I'd told him, but I reasoned that she didn't ask. She'd only asked about my family, and I hadn't told them, so technically, I didn't lie. But I guess it was a lie of omission.

Laying in bed that night, I kept replaying what had happened with Leah over and over in my mind. And I tried hard not to think about Jasmine, but that proved to be impossible because I found myself consumed by thoughts from our last conversation.

My day had started, filled with excitement because it was Friday, and I didn't have a class, so I was going home for the weekend. And I was beyond excited at the mere thought of seeing her. Because although we talked on the phone a lot, it wasn't like seeing and holding her. And her kisses were so sweet that I longed for them.

As soon as I made it into town, I called her immediately to see when and where we could meet. But as soon as she answered the phone, I knew something was different because she sounded distracted and subdued, and that wasn't like her at all. She was always upbeat and talkative unless something was weighing heavily on her, and she'd tell me what it was about. But when I asked, she said we needed to meet right then at a spot we'd met numerous times before.

I remember it was a cold, crisp day, and the wind was blowing pretty hard, but she insisted that we meet at a park near her house because she couldn't stay long. Her voice sounded sad, so I was anxious and concerned about what she was going to tell me.

When I got there and made my way to the secluded beach where we'd spent countless hours talking and holding hands planning our future, I saw her standing there wearing a short red dress and black books. I went where she was and put my arms around her, but I could feel that she was trembling, and she pulled away.

I also recall her looking down as she spoke softly, "Julian, I'm sorry, but I only have a few minutes to talk because I have to go home and finish packing. I don't know how to tell you this, but my father is expanding his company, and we're moving away." But she never said where.

I must've gone to sleep because when I woke up, it was daybreak, and I reluctantly got up. I wasn't going into work until around eleven, but I was going to call Leah at eight.

The past few days had been stressful, but this morning, I was feeling slightly better. Leah had forgiven me, and I was determined to be a man of my word and do better. Jasmine's twenty-first birthday and our missed wedding day were behind me, and I'd survived it. It had been a close call where my relationship with Leah was concerned, but we'd pulled through. And now I was feeling more like myself and determined to be a better fiance' and move forward.

Jasmine would always be the love of my life. But I was going to put the past behind me and concentrate on the present and the future. Leah was the woman in my life now, and I had to focus on her. She deserved to enjoy this momentous time in her life, but she couldn't do that if I was always screwing-up and bringing her down.

Showering quickly, I grabbed a bite to eat and called Leah, whose tone was still ice-cold, and I completely understood because I'd hurt her deeply.

"Hey, I thought that maybe we could go out to dinner tonight, or perhaps, I can come over because I want us to put the past in the past and move forward."

"Yeah, I want that too, so come over around seven, and I'll be ready."

"Okay, I'll be there."

Getting off the phone, I knew I had my work cut out for me. Leah was hurt and upset, and I'd caused her that pain. So, I was determined to make it up to her starting tonight; therefore, I was prepared to wine and dine her at The Grand Imperial Palace, one of the most coveted five-star restaurants in town, where they also had a lively dance floor.

A friend of mine is the owner, so I called in a favor for the best table in the house with a few special touches, and luckily, he said he could make it happen. It had only been open for six months, and Leah had been dying to go, but it was always packed. So, I'd suggested that we waited until the novelty had started to wear off and go. But now, it seemed like the perfect time to take her. And although I'd never eaten there physically, I'd been inside, and it was quite impressive. And I'd ordered takeout numerous times to support my boy and had raved to him about the delectable food. And that was the truth because it's delicious.

At work, nagging memories tried hard to infiltrate my thoughts, and I fought with everything in me to keep them at bay. I worked on my computer, but my thoughts did wander back to the last time Jasmine and I had met at the park. I recalled that she wouldn't look me in the eyes, and that was something she always did. She'd say, "Julian, I love the color of your eyes because I can see my reflection. I know you got them from your great, great grandfather, and that greenish-brown eyes skipped a lot of people before you. So I wonder how long it will be before your beautiful eye color shows up again?

But that day at the park, she kept looking down, no matter what I said or asked her. She'd just say, "I don't want to leave, but I don't have a choice because I'm only sixteen, and I have to do what my parents tell me. I never wanted it to be this way, but this is how it has to be."

A sudden buzzing noise startled me, but it was just my secretary reminding me that I had a meeting. And that was a good thing because I was experiencing the same emotions I'd felt the day Jasmine left. My heartfelt heavy, but that feeling somewhat subsided as I prepared for my meeting.

The meeting went well, and I decided to call it a day, so I could go home and get ready for dinner. This night was supposed to be a turning point for us, so I wanted and needed it to be perfect.

On the ride over to pick her up, I felt like we were going on our first date, and I wanted to make a good impression. It didn't feel like we'd been together for a year and a half. And that was because of what transpired on Jasmine's birthday. I'd gotten drunk and damaged our relationship. It hadn't been perfect, but we'd been okay.

Pulling up to her townhouse, I felt anxious because I was being eaten alive with guilt about everything that had happened, and I felt even worse because Jasmine was still on my mind.

I got out of my car slowly, and it felt as though I walked a mile before I made it to her front door, but in actuality, it was a very short distance from her driveway to the doorsteps. I rang the doorbell, and when she answered, she looked lovely in a short black cocktail dress with silver shoes and jewelry.

"Hey, Julian, come on in. I just need to grab my purse, and I'm ready."

Entering quickly, I closed the door quietly behind me. "Leah, you look amazing."

"Well, thank you, and you're looking mighty dapper yourself. I don't think I've ever seen that black suit before. It's nice."

"No, you haven't. It's new, and thank you."

"Alright, I'll grab my purse."

On the way to the restaurant, there were a lot of awkward pauses in our conversation, and I wished that I'd chosen a closer place to have dinner. But when we pulled up, Leah's eyes lit up, and that alone made it worth it.

"Wow, you remembered that I've wanted to come here since it opened, and bringing me here is very thoughtful of you. Exiting the car, I went to open her door and handed my keys to the valet.

An attendant opened the door and greeted us warmly. And I was getting ready to give my name to the hostess when I heard someone calling me. Turning around hastily, I saw my friend, Donovan, the restaurant's owner standing there.

"Hey, bruh, Leah, please follow me. Julian, I have your table ready per your request."

He led us to an elevated corner table located in an extremely secluded area of the restaurant, and there were the yellow roses and candles that I'd asked for. I knew it was crazy, but I still couldn't buy red roses for anyone other than Jasmine.

"Hey, Donovan, this is what I wanted precisely, so thank you, and I got you later."

"Bruh, I'm just happy that you're pleased, and Leah, you look nice. I hope you guys will enjoy your night." Donovan pulled out Leah's chair, and we both took a seat, and he walked away.

"Julian, thank you so much because I can tell that you're trying hard to make an honest effort to make things better, and that means a lot. And these yellow roses are beautiful. Maybe, this is finally our turning point." Her tone was much softer than it had been earlier, and some of the tension had dissipated.

The waiter came to take our order, and we ordered spicy blackened shrimp and lobster tartlets for appetizers. We also ordered an expensive bottle of red wine.

Our night was off to a good start, and we enjoyed our appetizers. We also enjoyed a specialty dish of delectable grilled lamb chops, creamy, zesty rice pilaf, and roasted parmesan asparagus. And the wine was perfect too.

"Hey, Leah, would you like to dance?"

Holding out her hand, she smiled faintly, "Yeah, I would."

Dancing, I held her close, but not too close because things were still a little bit strained, and I knew it would take a while for us to get back to where we were. But I felt like we were heading in the right direction.

After dinner, I took her home, and she invited me in for a nightcap. And after she changed clothes, we sat on the sofa to talk.

Running her right hand gently through my hair, she looked at me intently, "Julian, tonight was special. I love my roses, dinner was delicious, and I enjoyed dancing with you. And I want you to spend the night, but I think we should wait to have sex when we're at a better place than we are right now. Our wedding night is just a few months away, and I think if we wait until then, it'll be special. Are you okay with that?"

"Yeah, of course, that's okay. I just want to make things right between us." Reaching out, I grabbed her right hand and held it tightly." I know that I hurt you, and I'm sorry."

That night, we slept in separate bedrooms, and I think it was the best thing for both of us. Because we were both dealing with the fallout from what happened, and since it had only been a couple of days ago, I knew her wounds

were still raw. And my guilt was relentlessly eating away
at me because I felt horrible about what happened.

Chapter 7

Over the following weeks, things had gotten so much better between us that it felt good. I still thought about Jasmine daily, but I'd come to accept the fact that my future was with Leah. So, I tried hard to be the kind of man she deserved in her life. I'd started to feel a little enthusiastic about our upcoming wedding and the parties that were coming up.

 My family even mentioned that I seemed more at peace, and even Cathy was starting to cut me some slack where Leah was concerned. It felt as though we'd turned a significant corner because even my relationship with her parents had improved. And my parents and I were looking forward to the dinner-party that Leah's mom was planning.

And although I thought about Jasmine every day, I was gradually beginning to make peace with the past. I had to accept that she would never be a part of my life again, and I had to move forward and be okay with that.

So I worked extremely hard on my relationship with
Leah and started to feel a measure of excitement and
happiness about our wedding. I even helped to pick out
china patterns and silverware.

I knew there was a part of me that would always long to
be with Jasmine, but that was okay because I'd finally
accepted that she'd made a choice, and she didn't
choose me. And there was nothing I could do that would
ever change that. So I'd made great strides in accepting
what I couldn't change and embracing what I had with
Leah. I became way more attentive to her emotional
needs and caught a glimpse of a slightly more caring
side of her. So much so that she'd occasionally fix me a
good home-cooked meal.

I also became more engaged in the last minute wedding
details, and I was excited about our upcoming
honeymoon to Barbados. We weren't having sex, and I
was looking forward to that part of our relationship
again. So I was happy that she'd suggested waiting until
our wedding night because that had been the right call
for us. However, on rare occasions, I did rely on Mr.
Standbye.

Arriving at work the day of Leah's parents' dinner party, I
felt confident that we'd weathered the storm, and the
dark clouds lingering from the past had lessened their
hold on me. And the echoes and cries that had been
continuously ringing in my ears had been significantly
quieted, and now I only heard very gentle sounds that I

could peacefully accept and live with. So tonight would be a huge stepping stone toward uniting our families before the wedding, and I was looking forward to it. But then, my phone started ringing, and it was Cathy.

"Hey, Julian, I hate to bother you, but I need to talk to you right now because this can't wait. I'm at home." Her voice sounded funny, so she had me concerned.

"Alright, I'll be right over, but please tell me that everyone's okay." Wild thoughts had started to penetrate my mind, and my imagination was running wild.

"Yeah, well, you already know that mom and dad have taken today off, and they're fine. Moms' getting her hair done for tonight, and dad had to meet with a potential client over breakfast. Now, please drop whatever you're doing and head this way!"

"Okay, Cathy, I'm grabbing my laptop because I can finish up what I was doing over there. I'm on my way."

On the drive over, a million thoughts were running rampant through my mind. What in the world was so crucial that Cathy had to see me right now? My mind went to Brian because if he'd done anything to hurt her, I was going to track him down immediately and kick his ass in such a way that he'd never forget it! If this boy had done anything to harm my sister, he was in trouble!

As soon as I pulled up, I grabbed my laptop and saw Cathy, who was waiting on the front porch motioning for me to come in quickly. We entered the house, and as soon as she closed the door, she started talking.

"Hey, I need to ask you something extremely personal, and trust me when I say that if it weren't important, I wouldn't ask! Just please know this isn't easy for me."

Shrugging my shoulders, I stared at her, "Okay, well, ask away."

"Alright, but let's take a seat at the bar." As she headed toward the kitchen, I was hot on her heels, plopping down on a bar stool quickly, and she did likewise.

"Okay, Cathy, now what is this all about?

"Well, I'm going to ask you some personal questions, although I'm positive that I already know the answers. However, I want you to indulge me anyway."

"Do you remember back when we were young, and Jasmine and I used to have a lot of sleepovers?

"Yeah, of course, I remember that." Scratching my head, I was trying to figure out where this was going.

"Well, as you know, Jasmine always had a huge crush on you that started when she was about five, and you were ten. She'd always say, I love Julian, and I'm going to marry him someday. And she wanted to follow you anywhere and everywhere! Quite frankly, you couldn't turn for her. And everyone thought her crush on you was cute until she turned twelve. Then they didn't think it was that cute anymore because she'd filled out, and it was obvious that you'd started to take notice and liked her too."

"But Jasmine's parents, as well as ours, were concerned because you were seventeen, and she was only twelve, so they all felt that you were way too old and much more experienced than she was. So they started their relentless campaign to keep yall apart and enlisted me to help."

"You guys were never to be left alone under any circumstances, and she couldn't stay over anymore until you went off to college, so I had to stay over there."

"Come on, Cathy, you know I remember all of this, and you also know what a struggle it's been to put it behind me. So why are you bringing it up? Please tell me what this is all about!"

"Julian, just bear with me for a moment, please! Do you remember how heartbroken and upset she was when you started to date? She cried about it regularly, and you weren't any better because, on her first date, you followed them to the restaurant and the movies. And I knew then that you cared about her because she wanted to know your every move, and you wanted to know hers too. So I was continually being interrogated by you guys as well as our parents. They would tell me over and over again not to leave you two alone, and if I saw anything that didn't look right between you all, to break it up and let them know.

But right now, I want to focus on one night in particular about five years or so ago, when you came home unexpectedly from college, and Jasmine was spending the night because her parents had to go out of town on business. Mom and dad were on pins and needles trying to keep yall apart because Jasmine was in their care, and they were responsible for her."

"Was that planned for you to come home?"

Shrugging my shoulders, I shook my head, "No, it was just a coincidence. I came home because the weather was changing, and I needed warmer clothing. But we did plan for her to come to my room that night after everyone had gone to sleep because we wanted some alone time together."

"Okay, I've always wondered about that. Well, anyway, that night, I knew Jasmine had something on her mind, and I knew that something was you. Because she'd soaked in the tub forever, curled her hair, and put on makeup and perfume, but I'd promised our parents that I'd keep you two apart, and I meant it. I was determined to make sure that she stayed put. But you already know that once Jasmine made up her mind to do something, she was going to do it no matter what."

"It was thundering and lightning that night, so everyone went to bed early. But I look back now, and I believe she pretended to be asleep around midnight so that I would go. But when I woke up around three, she wasn't there, and I knew exactly where to find her. So I got out of bed and headed to your room to get her because I didn't want you guys to get caught. But when I opened my door, lightning flashed brightly, and I saw her across the hall coming out of your room. So I closed my door quickly and jumped back in bed, and she never knew that I'd seen her."

"The next morning at breakfast, you two were all smiles, and mom and dad were breathing a huge sigh of relief that it was day time. But mom was nervous, and it seemed like she may have suspected something had happened because you all kept making goo-goo eyes at each other, even more than usual, and she was anxious for you to go back to school. Quite frankly, she pretty much insisted that you go back that day and not wait until Sunday, even though it was still raining heavily. And she didn't like for us to drive in the rain."

"And I already knew that you and Jasmine talked a lot, but after that weekend, you were always calling her because your face kept popping up on her phone, and she was excited. She kept saying that not only would we be best friends for life, but sisters-in-law as well. "

"But then, all that suddenly changed, and she didn't act quite like herself anymore. And I knew she wanted to tell me something, but she never did. I'd ask her what was wrong, and she'd say nothing. I'm fine. But she also started to miss school and cheerleader practice."

"Then out of the blue, about two months after she'd spent the night over here, she and her family suddenly announced that they were moving, but no one would say where. Jasmine simply said, my father is expanding his business, so we're moving. I don't want to go, but I don't have a choice because I'm only sixteen, and I have to do what my parents tell me to do. But when I tried to talk to her about keeping in touch and visiting, she'd shut down."

"Yeah, well, she pretty much told me the same thing. She said that things change and don't always work out as we want them to. We were at the park, and she wouldn't look at me when we talked. And no matter how many times I asked where they were moving to, she wouldn't tell me." My voice was shaky because all those memories that I'd fought so hard to suppress and bury had resurfaced again, and I was dealing with various emotions that I couldn't control. The echoes and loud voices from the past were once again screaming in my ears. And I longed to go back in time! So the switch I thought I'd broken had been triggered again, and I found myself wanting to be with Jasmine.

"So, big brother, my next question is extremely personal, and I want you to bear in mind that I'm a grown woman when you answer, okay."

"Yeah, okay."

That night, when Jasmine came into your room, how far did things go between you too? And like I said before, I'm grown."

"I drew my gaze to the floor because regardless of what, Cathy was still my baby sister, and I didn't particularly want to discuss my sex life with her, "Well, things went a whole lot further than they ever should've, but we didn't plan on what happened. We just wanted to make out, but things got way out of hand, and I acted carelessly. But if anything had happened, I would've left school and married her, and I told her that. But she never mentioned it, so we were okay.

"Shaking her head profusely and wringing her hands, she looked at me, "No, Julian, y'all were never okay."

"What are you talking about? Of course, we were okay!" Tapping my fingers on the countertop, I stared at her trying to figure out what this was all about. Because she knew how hard I'd worked to move forward, and this would only take me back. And I didn't need that a few weeks before my wedding.

"Well, believe it or not, I ran into Jasmine this morning."

"What? Where? My heart was pounding so fast that I thought it was going to jump out of my chest, and I stood up?

"I met a friend very early for breakfast in a town over where Jasmine's grandparents live, and I went to a drugstore to buy a few things, and there she stood."

"Is she okay?"

"Now, that's a good question because she looked as stunning as ever. She had the perfect hair, flawless makeup, and she was dressed beautifully and fashionably as always. But she looked sad."

"Really?"

"Yeah, really, she was undoubtedly shocked to see me and unusually quiet, which is definitely out of character for her. You know how much she likes to talk and kid around, but today, she was quiet and withdrawn, although she did ask about you? She'd heard that you are getting married and asked if you were happy. She said, and I quote, "that's all I've ever wanted for him," and I could tell that she was trying hard not to cry."
"She was the next one to check out, and the cashier was trying to show her the quality of the pictures she'd developed for her, but Jasmine was fidgety and quite obviously ready to go. So she told the cashier that she was sure they were first-rate and grabbed them quickly.

Being in such a hurry, Jasmine didn't even wait on her change or receipt. She hugged me, only saying how good it was to see me and that she'd stay and chat, but she had to catch her flight. And just like that, she was gone.

"But her phone number was still on the register, so I remembered it and wrote it down quickly. The cashier said she was definitely in a hurry because not only did she leave her change, she left her picture too. She also said, your friend's little girl is adorable. I said, yeah, she is, and she's at the perfect age. To which she responded, yeah, my little girl is four too. We talked about our kids when she stopped by here yesterday."

"And then, I volunteered to give Jasmine her change, receipt, and picture. The receipt says Jasmine Kennedy, and that explains why you can't find her. I also know for a fact that Kennedy is her mothers' maiden name. I searched her area code, and it traced back to Seattle, Washington. But that all pales in comparison to what I have to show you! So please brace yourself!"

Reaching in her purse for something, she then held up a photograph of a beautiful little light skin girl with long dark wavy hair and greenish-brown eyes.

"Julian, this little girl is undoubtedly your daughter because she looks just like you, and you'd have to be blind not to see it. This beautiful little girl even has your eyes!"

"Yeah, I can see that she's mine!" My voice was shallow and shaky, and I'd started to tremble because I was utterly overwhelmed with emotion. Now I knew that the same night I'd taken Jasmine's virginity, I'd also gotten her pregnant.

"Hey, it's indisputable that Jasmine was pregnant when they left here. And I'd bet my last dollar that it was all Mr. Daniels' idea to leave and keep it a secret. She's his little princess, and he'd do anything to protect her. He'd move heaven and earth to keep her pregnancy a secret because he'd never want anyone to know that she'd gotten pregnant so young. That's why she said that she didn't want to go, but she was only sixteen and had to do what her parents told her. It was because she didn't have a choice!"

My knees were weak, so I fell back down on the barstool. "I'm a father! Jasmine and I have a little girl together, but I swear nothing like this has ever crossed my mind! I'd told her that if this had happened, I would've married her, so she should've told me! " With shaking hands, I reached for the picture, stared at it, and stuck it in my shirt pocket.

"But right now, none of that matters. The only thing that matters is finding them. Hey, let's see if we can find her profile listed as Jasmine Kennedy."

Grabbing my laptop with trembling, sweating hands, I turned it on quickly, waiting for it to load. Then I did a google search on Jasmine Kennedy, and a long list of names came up. I started sifting through them carefully, and on the third page, I spotted a profile that fit her perfectly. The age, birth date, and previous address left no doubt in my mind that I'd just located Jasmine Danielle Darrington, and I was trying to control my emotions. And in less than ten minutes, I'd accomplished something that I hadn't been able to do in years. I knew where she was because I had her full address, 2504 Society View Drive, Seattle, Washington 34418.

And with a little more effort, I was shown the layout of her subdivision that took me on a virtual tour of the upscale neighborhood and placed an arrow right over her front door. After years of trying, I'd finally located Jasmine. And the realization suddenly hit me hard that not only had I found the love of my life, but I'd just discovered that she's also the mother of my child.

Tears were welling up in my eyes, "Cathy, I have to go to them, and I'm leaving today! If I can't take dad's plane, then I'm booking a flight asap."

"Come on, Julian, you can't leave today because Leah's family is hosting a dinner party for you all tonight. It's a chance for the parents to get to know each other better, so you should at least go to that. Then you can talk to your fiance about this and fly out tomorrow. Besides, we

114

don't know that Jasmine flew back today. Maybe she was just making an excuse to get away from me." Standing up, she leaned on the bar.

"No, I don't want to hurt Leah! You know I don't! But I've been looking for Jasmine for years! And now, I know where to find her and our daughter. And I'm not missing another moment of my child's life for anyone or anything. I want to see them today, so I'm willing to take a chance that she flew back this morning!"

In an emotional frenzy, I called my father immediately, "Dad, you know, I wouldn't ask this if it wasn't an emergency, but I desperately need to use the plane this evening if possible. I wouldn't ask if it wasn't urgent."

"Yeah, of course, you can, but what's wrong? Because we're supposed to have dinner at your future in-laws tonight, so what's going on? Son, are you okay?"

"Yeah, I'm okay, but I won't be there. It's a long story, and I can't explain it to you right now, but I have to do this because I don't have a choice! And I'll be gone for a few days, so I'll take a commercial flight back."

"Okay, well, I'll call the pilot and have the plane ready by four, and you know, I'll pick up your slack at work. You just go and do whatever you have to do. And, I don't want to pry, but I have to log a flight manifest, so what's your destination?"

"I'm heading to Seattle, Washington."

"Alright, that's all I need to know, but please be safe and keep in touch with your old man."

"I will."

"Pressing the button to end my call, I turned to Cathy quickly, "I hear what you're saying, but I have to do this. I have a beautiful little four-year-old daughter, who I want to physically see and hold for the first time and be a part of her life. I don't know if things will work out with Jasmine, but I've never stopped loving her. I think about and miss her every day, and I need to find closure one way or the other. I understand that she was only sixteen when I got her pregnant, but that was years ago. So why hasn't she reached out to me? I can't understand why she chose not to tell me about our baby!"

"Julian, I understand, but what are you going to tell your fiance'? I'm not Leah's biggest fan, but I hate to see her get hurt." Sighing loudly, she sat back down at the bar."

"Hey, I don't want to hurt her either. Because I do care deeply for her, but I have to do this for me. I know Leah, her family, and friends will hate me, but I can't help that. Because at this moment in time, the only thing I can think about is seeing Jasmine and our daughter."

"I love this little girl already, and I've never seen her in person, nor do I even know her name. All I know is that I desperately want to see and hold her. So, I'm going home to get ready for my trip."

"Now, I realize that no matter how hard I've tried to stop loving Jasmine, I haven't, and I never will. In all honestly, I can't ever remember not loving her even when she was an annoying little girl who was always in my personal space. I remember at her fifth birthday party when she said that she loved me and wanted to marry me when she blew out her candles. I recall thinking even then, maybe someday. There's no one like her, and she'll have my heart forever."

"Yeah, you're right. Jasmine's something special, and I think about and miss her every day too. I'd love to have my best friend back in my life again, but right now, you need to talk to your fiance'. You need to tell Leah what's going on." Standing up, we embraced tightly.

I left, and when I got home, I immediately called Leah.

 "Hey, Julian, I stopped by your office earlier, but of course, you weren't there. And I've texted and called you several times but got no answer. What's going on?"

"I'm at home, and I need to talk to you about something that can't wait. Are you at your office?"

"No, I'm at home getting ready for dinner tonight, and I hope you are too."

Clearing my throat, I hesitated, "Leah, I'm sorry, but something has come up, and I can't make it. I'm so sorry!"

"What?" Please tell me you didn't say you can't make it! My parents are expecting your parents and us tonight! What in the hell is wrong with you?" Her voice was loud and shrill.

"I'm sorry, but I have to address something that can't wait."

"So, what am I supposed to tell my parents? What do I say to them?

"Leah, I'm sorry to put you in this awkward position, and I'll call your parents and apologize to them myself as soon as we hang up."

"No! Don't fucking bother! I'll tell them myself!"

Chapter 8

Our connection broke suddenly, and I went to pack for
my trip. Our time zone is three hours ahead of
Washingtons', so I was planning to see them tonight
because it would still be relatively early when I landed.

Quickly looking online, I booked a hotel room very close
to where Jasmine lived, and I also rented a car.

On my way to the airport, I was thrilled when my father
called to tell me that the arrangements had been taken
care of. It was just a matter of boarding the plane and
waiting to be cleared for take-off.

Having a little time to kill, I went to the airports' gift shop
and purchased the biggest pink and white teddy bear
that I could find, and I was a proud father when I told the
cashier that it was for my four-year-old daughter.

It was quite a challenge boarding the plane with my
luggage and carrying a huge bear, but I managed.

"Hey, Mr. Peterson, I've checked the radar, and it's storm-free, so we should have a smooth flight. And, we should be landing in Seattle in about four and a half hours, five at the most."

"Hey, man, please call me Julian because being addressed as Mr. Peterson makes me feel old." Chuckling when I said that, he did too.

"Okay, well, Julian, you can get buckled in and relax because we'll be taking off in twenty minutes. I just got the clearance."

"So, when are you planning to return home?"
"Truthfully, I don't have a definitive date, but you can fly back tomorrow if you'd like. I'll pick up your tab for room and board whenever you choose to stay tonight."

"That's very generous of you, but your father has already taken care of that. And I think I will fly back tomorrow because the following day is my tenth wedding anniversary, and I want to spend it with my true love."

"Well, congratulations, and allow me to pick up your dinner tab." Taking out two one-hundred-dollar bills from my wallet, I handed them in his direction."

"Nah, man, that's too generous, and I can't accept it."

"Hey, I believe in true love, and it seems as though you have that. And you're flying me to Seattle to reunite with mine, hopefully. I don't know how things will turn out, but you have given me hope. So please take it".

"Thank you, and I hope this will be the beginning of your life with her. I don't want to be too personal, but does she know you're coming?"

"No, she doesn't."

"Well, Julian, she must be something special, and I truly hope that things will work out the way you want them to. And once again, thank you."

"She is special, and you're welcome."

During take-off, I had a million and one thoughts running rampant through my mind. I kept thinking back to when Jasmine and I were growing up together, sharing holidays and birthdays. Our families were always doing things together, so our ties ran extremely deep. And we'd fallen deeply in love, and now, we had a baby girl conceived out of our love and passion.

And I remembered that on my twenty-first birthday, Jasmine was still fifteen, although Cathy had turned sixteen, so her birthday was fast approaching. I was away in college, and my birthday had fallen on a Wednesday, but I'd skipped school, and so had she. So I'd come home without telling my parents, and we'd met at the park near her house, and had a picnic laughing and taking pictures, as we planned for our future.

We also happily ate fried chicken and potato salad along with all kinds of fruits she'd bought at a nearby store. And I remember her walking back to her car and coming back with a beautiful white cake with blue icing, a twenty-one candle, and it had an inscription that read, "forever in my heart, I love my college boy." Leaning back in my seat and closing my eyes, I tried to control my emotions and prayed that Jasmine and our daughter were at home. I also prayed that Jasmine didn't have another man in her life. Because if she did, I'd be devastated all over again!

Upon landing, I picked up my rental, checked into the hotel, and headed to Jasmines. It was still relatively early, and I was extremely anxious to see them. Within thirty minutes, I was entering her large upscale subdivision, and my heart was beating like a drum as I passed one big house after another. I hadn't seen her in years, and I'd never physically laid eyes on our daughter, so I was filled with mixed emotions, ranging from happiness to being pissed off that she'd chosen to keep my baby away from me.

It was dusk dark when I pulled up to a big tan colored two-story house with brown shutters and exited my car, debating whether or not to carry the bear with me, but I quickly decided against it. So, I proceeded slowly to her front door, took a deep breath, and rang the doorbell.

Standing there, it felt like an eternity but was probably mere seconds before the door opened, and Jasmine and I were standing face to face for the first time in years. And I could see the look of pure shock etched across her beautiful face.

"Julian, how did you find me, and why are you here?" Cathy?" Visibly trembling, her voice was low and shaky.

"Yeah! Cathy! She saw your name on the receipt you ran off and left, and it said Jasmine Kennedy, so I looked you up! And I think you already know that we need to talk!"

"You really shouldn't have come because I can't go through this again! Please leave!"

"No, I'm not going anywhere, so you may as well accept that and let me come in."

As soon as she stepped aside, I entered quickly, pushing the door closed behind me.
Reaching into my shirt pocket, I took out the picture that my sister had given me and held it up, "I already know who she is because I can look at her and see that she's mine. But I just need to hear you say that she's my daughter. I need to hear it from you!"

Tears were lapping down her face as she stared at me shaking her head affirmatively, "Yeah, she's yours. She's your daughter!"

"What's her name?" Struggling within myself, I fought hard to control my emotions, but my voice was shaky. As I stood there, staring at the love of my life, desperately needing answers that only she could give me.

"Jordan, her name is Jordan Alexandria Kennedy. "

"I like Jordan, and you gave her the female version of my middle name Alexander. So thank you." Tears wanted to shed, but I struggled to hold them back.

"Yeah, I had to, and I listed you as her father on her birth certificate because I couldn't leave you off. You're her father!"

"Why didn't you tell me that you were pregnant? How could you keep my child away from me? I told you if that happened, I would marry and take care of you, and I meant it, and I thought you knew I did! So why didn't you tell me?" Fighting to stay calm, I tried hard to keep my emotions in check, but my voice was shaky and cracking.

"I wanted to tell you! I never wanted to keep her away from you, but I didn't have a choice! When I found out that I was pregnant, I was beyond scared, not so much for myself, but you." Visibly trembling, she looked directly at me with those piercing dark eyes that I'd longed for years to look into once again.

"I was only sixteen, and you were twenty-one, so I knew what that would've meant for you. I was underaged, and it would've ruined your life because the age of consent in Virginia is seventeen. No one would have cared that I came into your room, and I was all too willing to be with you and knew what I was doing. That wouldn't have mattered at all, and you would've been facing statutory rape. And I couldn't bear that, so I didn't tell anyone. I was trying to figure out what to do." Tears were streaming down her face, and I could feel her anguish as she stared at me.

"But I had horrible morning sickness, and I tried to keep it hidden. My dad was at work a lot, so it was mainly my mom who noticed. And I knew she suspected it because she kept saying, sweetie, you can confide in me about anything, and I won't judge you. Just remember that I was young once too, and things happen because nobody's perfect."

"Then, one morning, I felt nauseous, and my mom wanted to talk to me about something, but I couldn't concentrate because all I wanted her to do was leave, so I could be sick and lie down. When she finally left, I ran upstairs to my bathroom just in time, but when I came out, she was sitting on my bed waiting for me, and

I could tell by the way she looked at me that she already knew.

"She said, sweetie; I pretended to leave, so you could be sick and hopefully feel better. Do you think you're pregnant?"

"I shook my head, yes."

"Julian?"

"Yes, and I told her how sorry I was for disappointing her, but she was extremely nurturing and understanding. She just held me in her lap and rocked me like I was a little girl assuring me that everything would be okay. She said that I wasn't the first young girl to get pregnant, nor would I be the last. And I remember her saying that she loved me unconditionally."

"She asked if I'd had a pregnancy test, and I said no. She also asked if I'd told you, and I said not yet. And she said to wait until she talked to my father first. Then she took me to a doctor about seventy miles away, to a friend of hers, whose daughter had also gotten pregnant in high school. I took a pregnancy test, and it confirmed what I already knew, I was pregnant."

"Afterwards, she took me out for lunch, and she told me what my options were, but not having our baby never crossed my mind. I wanted our baby because I loved it already, and to me, it symbolized the love that we shared."

"That evening, when she told my father, he was so upset and angry that he broke down and cried. I'd never seen him so emotional and inconsolable before ever, and he blamed everything strictly on you. I tried to tell him that we were in love, but he didn't want to hear that."

"He said, and I quote, "this is why we tried so hard to keep you two apart because we were all afraid that something like this would happen. But I hold him solely responsible because he's a grown man, and he should've known better. So if you love him as you think and say you do, then you won't tell him because he's going to be locked up, as well he should be. If anyone finds out about this pregnancy, the privileged life that he's known will be over because he's going to jail!"

He also said that you were a tall, handsome, twenty-one-year-old man, and a lot of girls were undoubtedly throwing themselves at you. And for me not to think for a second that I was the only one you were sleeping with, but I was just the one who got pregnant. And that it was lust you felt for me, not love."

He said that you were in college enjoying every aspect of your life while I was carrying your child! And that broke my heart."

So the initial plan was for us to move away, and my parents would pretend, as though they'd accidentally gotten pregnant later in life. But I wouldn't agree to that because I didn't want my child thinking that I was its sister. I wanted it to have its mother, even if it couldn't have its father."

"When we first moved here, I longed for my past life and cried a lot, which wasn't good for the baby or me because my blood pressure kept going up. But after a while, I came to accept things as they were because I was pregnant and had to pull myself together. I needed to be strong and well physically and emotionally, so I could give birth to a healthy baby. And I finished up high school online."

"The night that Jordan was born, it was cold and wet, and I remember thinking, how badly I wanted you to be at the hospital with me because I was so scared. But I knew it wasn't by choice that you weren't there, so I held on to the thought that if you'd known, you would've been by my side. And that helped me to deal and cope with everything that was happening."

"I was in labor for hours, but it wasn't all that bad because I had an epidural and didn't feel any actual pain, just a lot of pressure. And she was a small baby weighing only six pounds, two ounces, but she gained weight quickly."

"By the time my eighteenth birthday rolled around, my father had mellowed out a lot because Jordan was his heart, and she had him wrapped around her tiny little fingers. He apologized for the way he'd handled things and said you had a right to know that you have a baby girl who's the spitting image of you. And that there was no way she could've passed as their child because if anyone who knew you saw her, they would know the truth. They'd know that we'd had a child together."

"So, he bought me a plane ticket to fly back home to tell you about Jordan. And on the flight there, I fantasized about us reuniting and living happily ever after. I was so excited and anxious to see you again because I couldn't wait to tell you about and show you our beautiful little girl, who looks just like you. I desperately wanted that fairy tale ending for us. I wanted romantic music playing in the background and the sun shining brighter than it ever had before, as we ran to each other and reunited."

"But when I got to town, instead of calling you immediately, I decided to grab a quick lunch. And when I walked into the restaurant, I saw you sitting there having lunch with some girl, and my heart exploded into a million tiny pieces. Because I was standing there just feet away from you holding Jordan, and I turned around and left because I didn't want to disrupt your life! I only wanted you to be happy, and you looked like you were! And I cried over what I'd seen and for what would never be. Because this wasn't a fairytale, and there wouldn't be any happily ever after for us. So I had to accept that our relationship was over and let the dream of reconciling go. And that realization stung like hell, and it still does!"

"I rented a hotel room and flew back here the following day, determined never to set foot in Richmond again. Simply telling my parents that when I got there, I'd changed my mind about telling you because too much time had passed."

"And I focused on giving our daughter the best life that I could provide her because I didn't want my parents to support us. I wanted to do it myself, so I started taking college courses online in technology, and I came up with some awesome apps and games that took off. Therefore, I started my own company, called J 3, symbolically representing the three of us. It's doing exceptionally well in the states and Japan, so I have to travel there from time to time. "

I bought this house and hired a nanny for Jordan. She's in pre-k, so I work from home while she's in school from eight-to-twelve. That way, I can do my work and spend as much time with her in the afternoon as I possibly can. But I also have Ms. Granger here a lot, and Jordan adores her because she's more like an aunt to her than a nanny."

"Did you send birthday cards to Cathy and me from Japan?"

"Yeah, I had to. I missed you all so much, and I couldn't let those milestone birthdays pass without acknowledging them, even though I didn't sign the cards."

"Yeah, well, that thought crossed both of our minds, but we thought we might have been grasping at straws because we wanted them to be from you."

"And when you came home and saw me with another girl, I wasn't dating her or anyone else at that time. Whoever she was, she was just a friend. I did eventually start dating, but I've never forgotten about you, not ever. I searched for you on any social media platform that I could think of, but it was as though you and your family had disappeared from the face of the earth. And that's because I was searching for Jasmine Danielle' Darrington, not Kennedy. I've looked for you since the day you broke my heart and left. You said this is how it has to be."

"If only I'd stayed when I came to see you, but now it's too late for us, and I want you to be happy. And I think you've found that without me because you're getting married in a matter of weeks. So as I said before, this is how it has to be because our timing has always been off." Tears were slowly lapping down her face as she continued to look directly at me.

"I'm sorry that you've missed so much of Jordans' life, but I promise that I'll never try to keep her away from you again, and you can have as big or small a role in her life and upbringing as you choose. I've shed a million tears because you weren't a part of her life. After all, I knew how much you'd love her. And I wanted to be a part of your life too, but that can never be. "

Walking over to her, I reached out and caressed her beautiful face ever so gently with my right hand wiping away tears, "No, I can't marry Leah when I'm still in love with and long to be with you. Jasmine, I've loved you for as long as I can remember. I loved you even when you were an annoying little girl who was always in my personal space. And then you grew into this incredibly beautiful, sexy, amazing woman who stole my heart, and now that I've found you again, I'm never letting you go. I love you, and I always will." Leaning in to kiss her, I heard a soft voice.

"Mommy, I want some juice, and my baby wants some too. We're thirsty."

Looking up at the staircase, I saw my beautiful little girl walking down wearing a short pink gown and pink and white bunny slippers, carrying a babydoll wrapped in a pink ruffled blanket. And my heart was pounding at the sight of my little princess, as she came and stood right beside Jasmine and waved at me.

"Hey, sweetie, you're beautiful. Trembling, I fought my urge to grab and hug her, but she didn't know me, and I didn't want to scare her.

"I know you." Holding her doll tightly, she stared at me.

"You do?"

"Yeah, you're the man in the picture by my bed. My mommy said you can't be with us."

"Jordan, I'm here now, and I want to get to know you. Is that okay? Warm, salty tears were running down my face into my mouth as I stared at her. This beautiful little hazel-eyed girl was a part of me, and my heart was overflowing with love,

"If my mommy says it's okay, it's okay with me. But why are you crying? My mommy gets sad and cries if I ask about my daddy, so I try not to bug her."

"Is it okay if I hug you?"

Shrugging her tiny shoulders, she looked at Jasmine again, " If my mommy says it's okay, then it's okay with me."

"Yeah, sweetie, it's okay."

She ran to hug me, and I bent down and held on to her for dear life. She started squirming and laughing, "You're squishing me like grandpa does."

"Okay, Julian, she needs to go to bed because the flight home wore her out. But tomorrow is Saturday, and you guys can hang out all day. I'll call Ms. Granger and let her know that she can have tomorrow off, and that works out because she needed to be off for something and could only stay for a little while anyway just because Jordan wanted her to.

"Hey, Jordan, I have something for you, and I'll be right back!" Rushing to my car, I grabbed her teddy bear, and when she saw it, her eyes lit up, and she gave her baby doll to Jasmine.

"Wow! This thing is bigger than I am! Thank you. I'm going to name it Pinky. Pinky the giant bear. I love it, and I think it's a boy. He'll love my room." Struggling and giggling, she grabbed Pinky and hugged him tightly.

"Hey, I'm going to get her some juice and tuck her in if you want to come."

"Sure, I'd love to." My heart was bursting with excitement to be a part of something so simple in our daughter's life.

"Okay, well, I'll get the juice."

Jasmine went into the kitchen and came back with the juice that she polished off quickly. And we proceeded upstairs with Jordan, who was struggling with her bear but refused to let us help her, which Jasmine and I found amusing, as we looked at each other smiling.

Eventually, we made it upstairs to the landing, walked down the hallway, and opened the door to Jordans' enormous bedroom that looked like it was fit for a princess. She had a white carriage bed with pink and white bedding and a pink canopy. It also had a make-up table, dollhouse, numerous dolls, and toys everywhere. There were also frilly pink curtains and pink and white rugs so that Pinky would fit right in. It would be any little girl's dream room. And I spotted my picture on the nightstand right by her bed, and I remembered the day that Jasmine had taken it, when we were at the park celebrating my twenty-first birthday, while we planned our future together, and now, we could finally have that.

Kneeling, Jordan started saying her prayers."Thank you for my mommy, my grandma, grandpa, Ms. Granger, my dolls, my toys, and Pinky. And thank you for letting my daddy come to see me, amen." Standing up quickly, she hopped into bed.

I was choked up and amazed that she knew who I was because we'd never actually told her that, yet she still knew!

"Jordan, how do you know that I'm your father?" As I stared at her, my heart was overflowing with emotion, and I could feel a connection.

"My eyes are like yours, and I look like you."

"Yeah, sweetie, you do look like me, and I love you."

Jumping out of bed, she hugged me, "I love you too, daddy." Tears were streaming down my face, and I looked over at Jasmine, who was shedding tears and joined us in a group hug until Jordan broke our embrace. And I could feel my heart swelling with an indescribable feeling of love and emotion.

"Mommy, let daddy spend the night, and he can eat pancakes with us in the morning. Can he please?" Hopping excitedly, she got back in bed.

"Sure, sweetie, if he can."

"I'd love to." My heart was pounding at the mere thought of staying here and having breakfast with them.

Tucking her in, after many hugs and kisses, we went back downstairs to finish our conversation.

"Jasmine, she's beautiful and so smart! She's the kind of daughter a father dreams of having! You've done an amazing job."

Walking over to her, I bent down, kissed her, and it was as though time had stood still. It didn't feel like secrets, time, nor distance had kept us apart because I knew that in her loving arms was where I was supposed to be.

It was the only place I longed to be. Our kisses grew more and more passionate as we were anxiously undressing each other and moaning softly.

"Mommy, daddy, I want to sleep with you all tonight. I'm too happy to sleep in my bed, and Pinky can't sleep either."

Looking up, we saw Jordan standing on the staircase landing holding Pinky and looking down at her parents, who were barely dressed, kissing, and touching all over each other. My shirt was off, and Jasmine only had on a matching yellow panty and bra set, and I'd unsnapped the bra, so she had to hold it on.

"Alright, sweetie, but please go back to your room, and daddy and I will be right up."

"Okay, come get me when y'all have clothes on, and we can sleep together."

As soon as she skipped excitedly back to her room, we couldn't help but crack up. I laughed until my side was hurting, as we got dressed quickly."

"Hey, my bag is still in the car, and I'll grab it because my daughter wants me to spend the night. I'll take a quick shower, and we can go to bed with her. Being in the same bed is how this night is supposed to be. Because I'm going to sleep with the love of my life and our daughter."

"Putting her arms around my neck, she gazed into my eyes, "Then, I want it to be just the two of us because I've dreamed and fantasized about our only night together for far too long. And I'm tired of trying to remember how good it felt to be in your arms because I want to live and feel it again. I want to be with you."

"Baby, I want to be with you too. That night, when we made love, in my heart, I committed to you forever, and nothing has changed. Jasmine, I love you."

After quickly retrieving my bag, we went upstairs, and I showered while they waited in bed for me. Jordan was so excited that she wanted Jasmine to pop some popcorn and make sandwiches and tea so that we could have a tea party, and she did.

We also played games with her into the wee hours of the morning until she finally fell asleep. Then, I carried her back to her room and tucked her in while Jasmine took a soak in the tub.

I was in the bedroom waiting on her when she walked in, wearing an extremely sheer, sexy black gown with a slit in the side, and my heart started pounding. Standing up, I walked over to her, "You're beautiful, and I've missed you so much." Putting my right hand on her face, I caressed it gently as we gazed deeply into each other's eyes.

"I bought this gown years ago because after our night together, I thought we'd have many more, but that didn't work out. And for years, I've dreamed about wearing it and being in your arms again. And tonight, my dream is coming true. Julian Alexander Peterson, I love you. I always have and always will love you."

Gently, breaking our embrace, she held up her left arm, and she had on the bracelet that I've given her on her sixteenth birthday. " I held on to this because I plan to give it to Jordan someday. I want her to know that when she was conceived, her parents were very much in love.

Taking the engagement ring off the bracelet, I finally placed it on her left hand, where it was supposed to be. "This engagement ring is only temporary, and it will be replaced and upgraded immediately. And her parents are still very much in love.

"No, I don't want an upgrade because this is the only ring I'll ever want, and I'm never taking it off."

Tears were in her eyes, and I bent down and kissed her ever so gently. "Jasmine Danielle' Darrington, I love you too, and I've also dreamed of this moment. I remember when you came into my room and got in bed with me, but we never meant for things to go as far as they did. But there we were with nothing or no one to hold us back. So you gave yourself to me, and I never have and will never forget how good you felt. And now, we're free to feel like that again."

Kissing ever so gently, I could feel the desire building in me as our kisses grew deeper, demanding, and more passionate. I was holding Jasmine as tightly as I could, and the perfume she had on was sweet and intoxicating. It had been years since I'd made love to her, and I desperately wanted to. No other woman had ever come close to making me feel like she did because she held my heart. Our kisses grew more and more passionate, and I started kissing her on her neck as she rubbed up against me. My entire body was aching with desire, and I had an erection that was crying out, literally begging for satisfaction.

Although at this moment, it wasn't just about sex, it was about love and feeling that powerful connection that surpassed even my understanding. It was loving someone so deeply and whole heartily that the mere thought of losing her again made my heartache. It was about healing a wound that only her love could heal. I now realized that I'd only been a shell of a man, existing, trying hard to move forward, when my heart and everything in me was aching, longing to go back, or at the very least to understand why she'd never contacted me.

But now, I had the answers to questions that only Jasmine could give me. I understood just how deeply she loves me because she was willing to sacrifice herself to keep me from harm. And she was ready to step into the shadows because she didn't want to disrupt my life. That's a powerful love, and although I'd tried to free my heart and love someone else, I realized that even though I was engaged to and cared deeply for Leah, my destiny was and always would be with Jasmine because she would forever have my heart.

As I slowly slid the tiny straps of her gown down over her shoulders, it hit the floor, and she was standing there wearing only sheer black panties that left almost nothing to my imagination. Her body was amazing and didn't look like she'd had my baby. Her breasts were firm and perky, and her stomach was as flat as an ironing board. She was sexy as hell, and I longed to make love to her.

She unbuttoned and helped me out of my pajamas, and soon, I was standing there wearing black briefs and sporting a very rigid erection.

Reaching out, she pulled down my shorts and caressed me gently, which drove me wild with desire because I craved her touch, and I needed for my broken heart to be healed and whole.

Gazing deeply into each other's eyes, I picked her up, and laid her on the bed gently, and got on top of her kissing her passionately as I moaned ever so softly. I moved down, kissing her on her neck and then her breast before I anxiously removed her panties. I started licking and kissing her thighs, and then I buried my head between her legs, tasting her sweet nectar. She was squirming and moaning softly just like she had that night, so many years ago, when we'd had sex and made Jordan.

"Baby, that feels amazing, and it's been so long. I love the way you make me feel." Her voice was raspy, and her breathing was accelerated as she arched her back and squirmed.

Moaning softly, I eventually moved up and started kissing her again, passionately, and I had to take her right then. "Are you on birth control?" Moaning with excitement at the thought of possessing her again.

"No, there's never been anyone else."

"Baby, I don't want to use a condom because I don't want anything between us. I just want to feel you like I did that night! I desperately want to feel that way again, and I promise I'll get up."

"The last time we didn't use protection, we made a baby." We were both softly moaning as we rubbed up against each other.

"I know, but we weren't planning on having sex. It just sorta happened, but this time, I'll get up. I love you, and I just want to feel you. You have no idea how much I need that. I need you more than you can ever know. I love you."

In the midst of this, we were kissing passionately, and when I penetrated her, it felt as though my heart had been healed and rejuvenated because I felt whole, happy, and complete. And that was something that I hadn't felt in years.

"Julian, you feel so good, and I've missed you. I love you so much." Moaning softly, she gripped my butt tightly and moved in perfect sync with me as I thrust hard over and over again, loudly rocking the bed and shaking the headboard.

"I love you too. You're everything to me." I was lost in the throes of unbridled passion when I felt that she was having an orgasm, and I knew that I was very close too.

"Baby, please tell me to get up." I was moaning as waves of pleasure ran freely through me. "You need to tell me to get up. I need to hear you say it, and you need to say it now! Say it! Please say it! Tell me to get up!" Deep groans were coming from within me, and I knew I was right on the edge of having an orgasm, but I didn't want to withdraw. And this was precisely how I felt all those years ago when I couldn't pull out in time because she felt so good, and it felt like déjà vu was striking again.

"You need to get up, and you need to get up now." She let go of my butt.

"Okay, okay, baby, I am." And I reluctantly did just before I ejaculated on her thigh and fell over on my back raptured in ecstasy and moaning loudly, as indescribable pleasure flourished through every square inch of me. Oooooh, that felt so good. Oooooh, Ooooooh, That felt amazing."

"Yeah, it did. So that's what an orgasm feels like! It's indescribable!" Ooooooooh, I love the way you make me feel." Glancing over, I could see that her eyes were closed as she moaned softly and bit her bottom lip in an incredibly sexy way.

She'd just laid her head on my chest when the doorknob started twisting, "Mommy, daddy, what are y'all playing?"

Thank goodness, the door was locked because we were sprawled out on the bed butt naked, and we didn't want our daughter to see us like this. It was bad enough when she'd seen us half-dressed, kissing and touching downstairs earlier.

Sweetie, we were just playing a game and got a little too noisy, that's all. Daddy and I will try to be quieter, so we won't wake you up, okay." Working hard to stifle her laughter, she covered her mouth, and I was doing likewise.

"But we were in bed together."

"Yeah, we were, but you fell asleep, and daddy and I weren't sleepy, so he carried you to your bed."

"Okay, Daddy, don't forget, mommy is making pancakes in the morning, and you'll like them. Good night."

Alright, sweetie, I'm sure I will, and Jordan, I love you."

"I love you too, daddy."

Chapter 9

After laughing for what seemed like hours about what happened, we made love twice more, and I did reluctantly use protection, but I certainly didn't want to.

"Hey, I'll do something about birth control Monday."

We laid in bed, basking in the afterglow of mind-altering sex, and my heart was overflowing with joy. It was as though our bodies were the perfect match because we fit together like a glove.

"Jasmine, did I hear you right when you said there hadn't been anyone else?" Running my right hand gently through her hair, I leaned over and kissed her on the forehead.

"Yeah, that's what I said. I've dated some, but never seriously, and I've never introduced anyone to Jordan because I didn't want to confuse her if it didn't work out. Kids need stability. Although I do have a friend named Paul, who I've been seeing for a little over six months, I told him that I want to take things slowly. And I promised him that he'd meet her soon.

The next morning, we were up early, showered, dressed, making pancakes, and playing games with Jordan, who was beyond excited.

"Mommy, why did you close your door last night? You've never closed it before. Is it because daddy sleeps with you now?"

Struggling hard not to laugh, I looked at Jasmine as she struggled to answer her. I could see her face blush.

"Yeah, sweetie, and we didn't want to wake you up while we played a game."

"Okay, but I could still hear you all jumping on the bed like I do sometimes, and I wanted to play too. Oops, I wasn't going to tell that." Giggling, she placed her hand over her mouth quickly.

Looking at each other, Jasmine and I smiled.

"Alright, sweetie, it's okay this time, but please don't jump on the bed. And we can play games and have tea parties but only before your bedtime, and sometimes later on the weekends, okay. You have to remember that you have a bedtime, but daddy and I don't."

"Okay, I'm still a little girl, but I still like playing games with you and daddy."

"Sweetie, mommy, and I like playing games with you too. We love you so much."

We ate delicious pancakes, and we did indeed play games and watch cartoons all day. And it was by far the best day of my life. I loved getting to know my daughter. It was crazy, but I felt as though she had always been a part of my life because there were no awkward pauses or breaks in our conversation. She was my daughter, and we were connected by the heart instinctively.

It didn't matter that we'd only met a few days ago because she was a part of me. And Jasmine and I were consumed by a love that had withstood time, distance, and heartache because it felt as though we'd never been apart. It had been years, but we were as in love and connected as we ever were. If anything, I loved her even more.

The following day my father called to check up on me.

"Yeah, dad, I'm fine. I haven't felt this good in years."

"Okay, well, you haven't sounded this good in years either. What's going on?"

"Hey, this is something that I can't explain over the phone, but I'll be home in a few days, and we'll have a lot to talk about."

"Okay, son, I just hope you know what you're doing! And I know you're not with Leah because she's been calling me and your mom trying to find out where you are. She even called Cathy, so you know she's upset because those two don't exactly talk on the phone. Is this business or what?

"It's not business, and that's all I can tell you. But right now, I have to go."

"Okay, well, I'll talk to you later. Your mother and Cathy said hello, and I get the feeling that your sister knows what's going on, but she won't utter a word."

Monday morning, I got to meet Jordans' nanny, Ms. Granger, who was a very gregarious middle-aged lady who knew that I was Jordan's father before Jasmine could utter a word. She took her to school, and Jasmine and I spent time filling in blanks in our lives and rediscovering why we'd fallen in love. And why, we still were.

I also found out that her parents were on vacation in Florida and would be back in a couple of days, and they were aware that I was here.

Showing me pictures of when she was pregnant, I also saw countless images of Jordan as a baby. And she was a beautiful, chubby-cheeked little girl with a head full of dark hair. She'd chronicled her pregnancy over the months and never got all that big. And although she looked a little sad in most of her pictures, she still looked radiant and beautiful.

We hung out until it was time for her to see her doctor about birth control, which made me happy. And when she returned home, Ms. Granger had dropped off Jordan, and we were attempting to cook a chicken casserole for dinner that turned out to be pretty good. And being in the kitchen goofing around and cooking with our daughter was priceless. She was a great little helper, and I wouldn't trade that time with her for anything in the world.

The following day, I talked to Jasmine about flying back home with me, so my parents and sister could meet Jordan, and she happily agreed, so she contacted her school and Ms. Granger while I booked our flight. And I was thrilled because I couldn't wait to introduce them to Jordan and announce that Jasmine and I were back together for keeps. And I owed them an apology for conceiving a child in their home.

Also, as a man, I knew there was something else that I had to do. I had to talk to Jasmines' parents about everything that had happened and try to rebuild my relationship with them. They would be returning the following day, and I planned to talk to them immediately. And although I knew that explaining everything to her father would be difficult, I prayed that we could reconcile and be a family again like we were before this all happened.

Very early, the following morning, Ms. Granger had picked up Jordan for school. And Jasmine had gone upstairs to shower, instructing me to answer the door if the doorbell rang because she was waiting on an essential package from Japan that was supposed to be delivered this morning. She didn't want it left on the porch.

So when the doorbell rang, I answered it quickly and found myself standing face to face with a relatively tall, clean-cut looking guy dressed in khakis and a red polo shirt, holding flowers, who wasn't the postman and didn't appear happy to see me.

"Who are you?"

"Julian, and you are?"

"I'm Paul, Jasmines' boyfriend. Where is she?"

"She's upstairs." He more or less walked past me, and I closed the door only to turn around and see him picking-up a picture of Jordan from a nearby table.

"So looking at you and a picture of Jasmine's daughter, I'm quite sure you're her father because there's a striking resemblance with the eyes and all."

"Yeah, I am."

"Well, although I haven't had the pleasure of meeting her as of yet, I plan to soon. Because Jasmine and I have become extremely close, and I would hope that won't be an issue. I know she's very protective of her, and I respect that. I also know how some fathers are about having another man around their kid, especially a daughter. So, if you don't mind answering me, how long will you be here visiting her?"

"Hey babe, I thought I heard the doorbell ring. Was that my package?"

Looking up, I saw Jasmine bouncing down the stairs with her hair in soft curls, wearing a sheer provocative red gown, and she quickly put on her robe when she saw me standing there with Paul.

"Okay, Jasmine, I guess he's why you kept putting off introducing me to your daughter! And it also explains why you wouldn't sleep with me! So how long has this been going on behind my back?" His tone was loud and accusatory.

Before I could speak, Jasmine looked at me and shook her head, no," Please don't!"

"Paul, it's not like that. Julian and I only reconnected and reconciled a few days ago, and I was going to tell you when you got back in town. We haven't seen each other in years."

"I've texted and called you several times, and you never responded or picked up even once. So I stopped by to make sure that you're okay, and I can see that you are. You're doing just fine shacking up with him!." Glaring at her and then at me, he threw the flowers on the floor and stomped them repeatedly.

"Paul, I'm sorry. I never meant to hurt you."

"No, it's okay because I think this is how you've always wanted it to be! Some people can't let go or get over their first love!."

He turned quickly, opened the door, and slammed it forcibly as he angrily exited, causing several pictures to shake on the walls.

"I never wanted to hurt him."

Reaching out, we embraced, "Yeah, I know because I feel the same way about Leah, but this is our destiny." And as awkward as that encounter had been, I knew it would pale in comparison to the one that I'd eventually have with my fiance', who I hadn't even called since I'd been away.

The doorbell rang again, and it was the postman delivering Jasmines' package.

The following morning, Ms. Granger picked up Jordan, who had a field trip and wouldn't be home until three. And that was a good thing because Jasmine's parents were coming home this morning around ten, and I wanted to talk to them.

Jasmine and I hung out and made love all morning until her parents called to let her know that they were back in town, settled in, and we could come over whenever we wanted to.

"Hey babe, I already know that your parents are still upset with me, and I can't blame them. I just hope that we can get beyond it, so let's go.

When we rang their doorbell, my knees felt wobbly because I didn't know how Mr. Daniel would react to seeing me after all these years. Maybe, I had a lick or two to my head coming or perhaps a black eye and a busted lip!

The door opened, and her parents were standing there. Her mom was smiling, but her father didn't exactly look pleased to see me, and I certainly understood.

"Hey guys, come on in. Julian, it's nice to see you. Reaching out, she hugged me.

"Mrs. Carla, it's nice to see you too."

Upon entering and closing the door behind me, I reached out to shake her father's hand, and he did likewise. But there was a lot of tension in the air. I'd known him all my life, and I'd never experienced that with him before. But I fully understood because I was his godson who at twenty one had gotten his sixteen-year-old daughter pregnant.

"Hey, mom, I need to talk to you about something, and maybe Julian and dad can talk too." After giving me a quick peck on the cheek, she walked away with her mom.

"Mr. Daniel, I know you're still upset with me, and I can certainly understand why. But if you don't mind, will you please hear me out."

"Yeah, I'll listen. Let's go downstairs and talk."
With him leading the way, I followed him down to an enormous room, to what I surmised was his man cave because it had a huge flat screen tv on the wall, a pool

table, a small refrigerator, and dark leather furniture. And there was also a pinball machine.

"Alright, Julian, please take a seat, and I'll listen to what you have to say."

Taking a seat on the sofa, he sat in a matching recliner directly across from me, staring intently.

"Mr. Daniel, I'm deeply sorry for sleeping with Jasmine while she was underage. But I want you to know that it only happened once, and we agreed that night it would never happen again until she was of age. But please understand that I was deeply in love with her then, and I still am. I had no idea that she'd gotten pregnant, and I would've married her had I known."

"Because I told her that if that happened, I would've come out of school and married her, and I meant it. Mr. Daniel, I love your daughter, and I always will."

"And now, finding out that I'm the father of a little girl, I can understand and appreciate even more why you chose to protect her because I'd do anything to protect Jordan. So, I'm asking you to please forgive me."

Nodding, he stared at me, "Son, the result of your night together is my beautiful little granddaughter, so there's no way that I can stay angry with you. Because if not for that night, we wouldn't have Jordan, and that little girl is our heart. And when I look at her, I see you, and looking

156

at you now, I see her. That precious little girl looks just like you."

So, yeah, I accept your apology, and I owe you one for making Jasmine keep quiet about her pregnancy because you deserved to know the truth. So, I'm sorry too. And as angry as I was at you, I wanted to protect you also because regardless of what I said, I didn't want you locked up. You're my godson, and I do love you like a son."

We stood up and met halfway to shake hands but also ended up embracing briefly.

"Sir, I love you too. And I know this isn't exactly the order that this is supposed to take place, but I'm asking for your daughter's hand in marriage. I promise you that she and Jordan will be well cared for because I love them more than words can ever say. They're everything to me."

"Okay, but aren't you already engaged to be married in a few weeks?"

"Yes, sir, but I'm going to call it off because Jasmine is the love of my life, and I've been looking for her since the day you all left town. And now that I've found her again, I'm never letting her go because this is our destiny. Mr. Daniel, I love your daughter!

"Alright, so how are your parents and sister doing? We miss them, and we might be heading that way in a couple of weeks or so. The people who are renting our house are moving out of state in a few months. And now that all of this is out in the open, we might move back there. We like it here, but Richmond is home."

"Yes, sir, my parents miss you guys too. We all do."

We went back upstairs to find Jasmine and Mrs. Carla, and they were anxiously waiting on us. And it was apparent that they were holding their breath to hear how our conversation had gone because they were standing with their arms folded, looking extremely tense.

"Well, Carla, I think wedding bells will be ringing soon, and I'll be happy to hear them because our daughter and our godson are getting married.

Tears were running down Jasmine's face as she ran to hug her father. "Thank you for understanding that we were and still are in love."

Walking over to her mom, I hesitated as I searched my mind for the right words to say, "Mrs. Carla, I'm sorry about everything that happened." I was getting ready to say something else, but she cut me off.

"Julian, sssh, we have Jordan, and the two of you are back together, and that's all that matters."

Taking seats, we sat and reminisced about happy times gone by and looked forward to new ones to come. And when we finally left there, things were good.

"Hey, that went a lot better than I thought it would've. And like I told your father, I understand why he felt the need to protect you because I'm going to be the same way about Jordan. I'll do anything to protect her, and I definitely wouldn't approve of the age thing. So I guess that will make me a hypocrite, but so be it because there's no way in hell that I'd approve of a grown man dating our sixteen-year-old daughter since you can't look into someone's heart and know how they truly feel. So, I'd kick his ass and run him off with a quickness! But I was and always will be in love with you."

Reaching out, she hugged me tightly, "Yeah, I feel the same way."

Chapter 10

When Ms. Granger dropped Jordan off after her field trip, she was exhausted but excited to tell us about the animals she'd petted at the zoo. She ate dinner; Jasmine bathed her, and she went to sleep immediately.

After showering together, we tried hard to make up for time lost. Although, we chose to make love on an air mattress on the floor rather than disturb Jordan because she was dog tired and needed to sleep. So this way, we could express ourselves without having to worry about the bed squeaking or the headboard shaking. We could and did get buck wild.

The following day was Friday, and we would be flying out Saturday at ten-forty five heading to Richmond, and I was beyond excited.

Jordan was at school, and I was in the kitchen when I heard the doorbell rang, and I heard Jasmine answering it.

"Are you Jasmine Kennedy or Jasmine Darrington?"

"Yeah, and who are you?"

Listening carefully, I heard a very familiar voice, "I'm Leah, Julian's fiance'! Is he here?"

"Yes"

"Well, may I speak to him, please?"

"Yeah, sure, come in, and I'll get him."

Facing Leah was my moment of truth, so I went into the family room where they were and stood close to Jasmine.

Glaring at me with dagger eyes, Leah placed her hands on her hips and rocked from side to side, "Okay, Julian, I need some answers, and I need them now! Why are you here with her when you're engaged to me?"

"Leah, how did you find me?'

"I finally picked up your laptop, and for the first time since we've been together, you didn't bother to lock it. So I simply pulled up what you'd been looking at, and I discovered that you've been looking for Jasmine for years. I also saw her address, and that you'd booked a hotel room very close to here and rented a car. You left me a complete roadmap to her doorstep, but it took me a minute to discover it. So what's going on? Are you sharing a bed with her?"

"Hey Julian, I'm going upstairs and let you and Leah talk privately."

"No, please don't leave on my account! After all, this is your home, and it appears it's where my fiance prefers to be! And being that you've always been at the center of our issues, by all means, please stay!" Her tone was furious and emotional, and I could see the hurt in her face.

"Jasmine, when is your birthday?"

It's July eighteen, why do you ask?" Looking perplexed by the odd question, she glanced over at me.

"Oh, I asked because I just thought about something that happened one night, when for the first time, Julian kissed me passionately, but he called out your name. So I knew there was something significant about that date.

Because I'm pretty sure that he's never been drunk before in his life, but that night, he drank so much that he thought I was you. And you'll probably be happy to know that we never really had sex all that often, and it most definitely lacked passion. It was more like something; he felt obligated to do! He'd touch me, but he didn't want to because he wanted to be touching you! So you see, even though you weren't physically there, you've always been present!"

"So I'm asking you again, are you sleeping with her?" Her tone was loud and demanding as she glared at me and folded her arms.

"Yeah, I am."

"Okay, well, at least you have the decency, to be honest about playing house with her!"

Looking around and seeing a picture of Jordan, she walked over and picked it up quickly, " Julian, is this little girl your daughter?" Her hands were trembling as she stared at the picture. "She looks just like you, and the way I imagined our daughter would look. She's yours, isn't she? You have a daughter!"

"Yeah, she is."

As she stared at me, tears were flowing freely down her cheeks, "Why didn't you tell me? We've talked about children, and you've never mentioned having a daughter. Why didn't you tell me?'

"He didn't tell you because I didn't tell him! So, it's not his fault!"

"What? Why wouldn't you tell him about his child? He told me that you all were deeply in love, so why in the hell, didn't you tell him? If you loved him, then you would've told him!"

"I always have and always will love him! And as long as he understands and forgives me, that's all I can ask for! Now that's all I'm going to say on the subject." Her tone was shaky, and she looked nervous. And I knew it was because, once again, she was afraid for me.

"I still can't comprehend any logical explanation you could give to him or anyone else as to why you kept such a life-altering secret! Keeping his child away from him is incomprehensible to me! She's his flesh and blood, and he deserved to know!"

She kept staring at Jordan's picture, and I knew the exact moment that it dawned on her why Jasmine hadn't told me. Because her mouth flew open, and she looked over at her wide-eyed staring in disbelief.

"Oh my God, you were Cathy's best friend, and she just turned twenty-one several months ago. And this little girl appears to be about four or five, and I'm going to assume looking at you that you and Cathy are roughly the same age. So that means that you would've been underage when Julian got you pregnant. You had to be around fifteen or sixteen, and he was a grown man. You were jailbait, and he fell for you and got you pregnant. Wow! I can't believe this!"

"So, I suppose your parents snatched you up and brought you here to have your baby without telling him. And neither one of you has to answer that because I can look at your expressions and know that it's true. You two were star-crossed because of your age. Julian was a grown man sleeping with somebody's child!" Tears were streaming down her face as she sobbed loudly and openly. I can't believe this!"

"When he said that you had been Cathy's best friend, it didn't click with me about the age thing because I was thinking adults. But now, I can see the dynamics because you were a child, and Julian probably would've been charged with statutory rape. And I would imagine that thought certainly came to mind!"

She kept looking at the picture, "What's her name?"

Her name is Jordan. Jordan Alexandria Kennedy."

"Okay, well, I see you were thinking about Julian when you named her. So you were in love with him, and I guess you still are."

"On my flight here, I'd convinced myself that I hated you. Quite frankly, I blamed you for everything wrong in my life. But now that I'm here and have an understanding of what happened, I can only imagine how hard this had to have been for you at such a young age. You had to leave a man who you were still in love with and come here to have his baby without him knowing."

"I want to hate you, I really do, but I can't. And what's even crazier is that I can't even hate Julian for coming to find you! How pathetic is that?" Tears were streaming down her face as she set the picture back down.

"I think I'd like to meet Jordan if that's okay?"

"Well, she isn't here at the moment, but she should be home in about an hour, and you're more than welcome to stay. In fact, why don't you stay and have lunch with us? I know this can't be easy for you, and I'm sorry."

"No, it isn't, but I'll be okay. And I suppose it's pointless for me to hold out any hope that Julian and I will be getting married despite this. But, I think I knew that the moment I saw he was flying here to see you. And in doing so, he found out that he's the father of a beautiful little girl. So, I have to accept that this is where my fiance wants to be! He's always wanted to be with you!"

"I only ask for one thing, and that's to be able to tell my family and friends that I was the one to call off our wedding after he discovered that he has a child from a

past relationship years ago. Because anyone who
knows me knows that I've never wanted that, but now, I
look at how selfless you've been and how selfish I've
been. So maybe, I need to reevaluate some things in my
life. But before I do that, I'm going to be selfish one
more time and mislead people about this situation.
Because I don't want anyone to know that Julian chose
this path, so I have no choice but to take another. Can
you all give me that?" Tears were lapping down her face
as she held her head back.

"Of course, that's fine. Leah, I never meant to hurt you,
and I hope you know that."

"Yeah, I do, and I'm giving this back to you because it
means nothing any more!" Pulling off her engagement
ring, she placed it on the table by Jordan's picture.

Then the three of us went into the kitchen, sat down,
and talked as Jasmine prepared spaghetti, green salad,
and garlic bread for lunch.

She also explained how afraid she'd been for me when
she realized that we were pregnant. And in the process,
she explained why she'd never contacted me after she
became of age. And that it was because when she'd
flown home to tell me, she'd seen me with someone
else and didn't want to disrupt my life. Only to find out
now that she'd completely misread the situation
because I wasn't involved with anyone at that time.

Shortly after that, we heard the front door open and close, and Jordan came bouncing through the doorway carrying a picture followed closely by Ms. Granger, who spoke politely and left immediately.

"Mommy, Daddy, look at the new family picture that I drew. Is it okay if I show it to the lady?"
She waved at Leah, who was seated at the bar.

"Hello, sweetie, you're a beautiful little girl, and you look just like your father."

"Thank you. Are you staying with us too? My daddy sleeps in my mommy's room, and you can sleep in Ms. Grangers' room because she's not here. It's big, but not as big as mine or my mommy's."

"No, sweetie, I'm just a friend of your dad's, and I'll be leaving soon."

Do you want to see my picture?"

"Sure, I'd love to."

"Daddy, is it okay if I stand by the lady?"

"Yeah, sweetie, it's fine."

Skipping excitedly, she showed Leah the picture, "This is my mommy, my daddy, and me. My name is Jordan, my mommy's name is Jasmine, and my daddy's name is

Julian. He's going to live with us now." As she heard
those words, I could see the pain etched across Leah's
face.

"What's your name?"

"My name is Leah."

"Why are you so sad?"

"I'm okay."

"When my mommy is sad, I give her a big hug. Would
you like a hug?"

"Sure, that would be nice." They hugged, and I could
see that she was trying to fight back the tears, and I felt
terrible. But I could also see a faint smile as she pulled
on Jordan's long ponytail.

"Thank you, Jordan, I needed a big hug, and I feel better
about a lot of things." Breaking their embrace, Jordan
skipped over to Jasmine. "Mommy, I'm ready to eat."

"Okay, sweetie, I'm going to take you upstairs, change
your clothes, and we can all sit down for lunch shortly.
And that way, daddy and Ms. Leah can have a little time
to talk."

"Alright, guys, we'll be back downstairs in ten minutes or
so. Leah, please feel free to get yourself something to

drink. There's tea, water, and juice, and I'm sorry that I didn't offer sooner."

"Okay, thank you."

When they ascended the staircase and stepped on the landing, Leah looked at me intently, "I never thought I could twist my tongue to say this, but I like Jasmine. I can see why you love her because she's caring and quite pretty. And she hasn't tried to rub this situation in my face, like a lot of women would do. There's no smugness, or he wants me attitude because she's shown me nothing but understanding and kindness."

"And, it's amazing how much Jordan looks like you. If I'd seen her somewhere on the street, I would've done a double-take. She's a beautiful, intelligent, smart little girl, and I'm happy that she's in your life now. And I promise that I'll never tell anyone that Jasmine was underage when you got her pregnant. You have my word on that."

"Thank you, and I'm so sorry for hurting you. Please forgive me and know that I will always care about you."

They came back downstairs, and we all sat down to eat, only to discover that Leah's flight back home was tomorrow at the same time as ours, so we'd all be flying back to Richmond together.

When she left, we packed our clothes to get ready for our trip, and I was extremely excited to be flying home

with the love of my life and our little girl in tow. But I
knew that I'd temper my enthusiasm tomorrow because
I didn't want to hurt Leah any more than I already had.
And Jasmine, being the person that she is, said the
same thing.

Later that evening, I called my parents and told them
that I'd be home the next day and wanted to come over
to talk to them about something important. And I also
texted Cathy and asked her to be at home.

Awkwardly, the next morning, we sat together at the
airport waiting to board our flight. So, we were all a little
uncomfortable, but Jordan was chirping away excitedly
about flying again, which helped ease the tension
somewhat. And it was a huge relief when we heard that
our flight was boarding. But as luck would have it,
though, we had to sit in cross proximity, but we were in
first-class, so that helped because the aisles were wide
and spacious.

And when we finally landed, I rented two cars. One had
a booster seat for me to take Jordan to meet my
parents, and Jasmine drove the other one to follow Leah
to my house to help her pack any belongings she had
there. Then she'd meet us at my parent's later.

The traffic was a little heavy, but we eventually pulled up
to my parents. And I was thrilled to help my little girl out
of her booster seat and carry her to my parents' front
door.

"Daddy, where are we?" Rubbing her eyes, she appeared tired and sleepy.

"Sweetie, this is where I grew up."

Opening the door, I was still carrying Jordan when I went to find my family, who was seated at the kitchen table. My mom's mouth dropped wide open, and she gasped when she saw us standing there and stood up quickly.

"Oh, my God, Julian, she has to be your daughter because she looks just like you." Speaking in a high pitched voice, she appeared excited.

"Yes, mam, she is."

"Son, why didn't you tell us?"

"Mom, I didn't know."

Rushing, she came and stood in front of us, "You're such a beautiful little girl. What's your name?'

"Jordan "

"That's a pretty name." Tears were gently lapping down her face, and I looked over at my father, and he had teared up too. But Cathy was smiling widely.

I put her down, but she clung very tightly to me.

"Jordan, sweetie, would you like some cookies and milk?

"Yes, please. My mommy only lets me have two, but she's not here, so if you give me three, I won't tell."

That broke the tension, and everyone laughed hysterically, but Jordan, who just looked around the room as though, she was trying to figure out what was so funny.

"Okay, sweetie, you may have three?"

"Jordan, this is your grandma and grandpa."

"I already have a grandma and grandpa." Appearing confused, as she looked at them, she turned and looked up at me.

"Yeah, sweetie, those are your mommy's parents, but these are mine, so you have two more, and that's your Aunt Cathy over there waving at you.

"But what should I call them?"

My mom knelt in front of her, "Jordan, what would you like to call us?"

"My friend Timmy calls his grandma, Meme, and his grandpa, Paw Paw."

"Sweetie, that would be perfect, and Meme is going to get you some cookies and milk. And yes, you may have three. What's your mommy's name?"

"My name is Jordan, my daddy's name is Julian, and my mommy's name is Jasmine?"

"My parents stared at me with their mouths gaping wide open, "Yeah, that Jasmine, Jordan, is our little girl." My heart was filled with love and pride as I looked at my daughter.

"That's why they disappeared?! Gasping, she stared at me.

"Mom, please, let Jordan have her snack and lie down for a nap, and then we can talk. We had a long flight from Seattle, and she's tired."

"Yeah, of course. Jordan, do you want peanut butter or chocolate chips?"

"Chocolate chips, please."

"Okay, chocolate chips, it is."

"Okay, sweetie, after you finish your snack, Aunt Cathy is going to take you to your father's old room to take a nap, and you can look around and see if it looks familiar since this is where this all started." Giggling loudly, she winked at me, and I dropped my head.

"My daddy sleeps in my mommy's room, and they play games all night because I can hear them jumping on the bed, but they won't let me play. Because I have a bedtime, but they don't." I could feel my face flushing as my daughter hilariously and innocently outed me.

"Well, Jordan, I know your mom was in your daddy's room once, and I don't think they slept then either."

"Were they playing the game they play at home? I saw them from the stairs, and they were playing a kissing game while they took their clothes off." Covering her eyes quickly, she giggled.

Hysterically laughing and shaking their heads, my parents and Cathy pointed at me, and I drew my gaze to the floor quickly.

"What's so funny?"

"It's nothing sweetie, we all know your mom, from when she was a little girl like you, and that sounded like something she would've said." My father's voice was filled with emotion as he reached out and tugged on her ponytail.

"My grandpa says, I'm a handful like my mommy was at
my age. " Innocently, shrugging her shoulders,
"Whatever that means.

Looking around at each other, we all laughed again.

"Daddy, I'm sleepy, and I want to take a nap with PInky.
I ate all my cookies and drank all my milk."

"Okay, sweetie, I'll go get him. I retrieved Pinky, and
when I came back into the house, my parents were
hugging and kissing all over Jordan, who was giggling
loudly and squirming, and my heart was overflowing with
joy.

Cathy took her upstairs to my old bedroom, and when
she came back downstairs, we all sat down to talk.

"Mom, dad, first of all, I want to apologize for everything
I did under your roof and little sister that includes you
too. I'm sorry because that was extremely disrespectful."

"So, I guess the hint that Cathy was throwing about
Jasmine getting pregnant in your bedroom is true."

"Yes, mam. It's true. " Gazing at the tabletop, I tried hard
not to make eye contact with her.

Was this the weekend it stormed so bad, and you came
home unexpectedly from college, and Jasmine stayed
here because her parents had to go out of town on

business? Because I always felt funny about that night. And the only reason I didn't get up to check on you guys was that the weather was horrible, and you all know that I'm terrified of lightning. And perhaps that was a good thing.

"Yes, mam, but like I told Cathy, we didn't plan it. And we were only together once, so it happened that night. And if I'd known that she'd gotten pregnant, I would've married her. I've seen and apologized to her parents as well, and we're back on track.

"And I understand why her father took her away. He did it not only for her sake but for mine as well because we all know what probably would've happened to me for getting an underage girl pregnant. And I'm not proud of that, but I'm extremely proud of and thankful for our daughter, so it's a night that Jasmine and I will never regret!"

"Her parents asked about you guys and will probably be coming to visit in a few weeks because they never actually sold their house. They're just renting it, and the tenants are going to be moving out very soon. So, who knows, they might move back here."

"Son, we accept your apology, and we love Jordan already. She's a beautiful little girl, and your mother and I are as proud as any grandparents can ever be. We'd also love to see Daniel and Carla again, and hopefully, we can pick up where we left off because they're our best friends. After all, we miss them terribly. So, where's Jasmine?"

"She's at my house, and she'll be here shortly."

"So Julian, I have to ask, are you still marrying Leah?"

"No, mom, that's over. Jasmine and I were deeply in love all those years ago, and we still are. She's my destiny, and I'm going to marry her. I would've married her then had I known!"

"Okay, but when are you going to tell Leah?"

As I leaned back in my seat, they all stared at me.

"Well, she already knows because she followed me to Seattle, and believe it or not, we all flew back here together."

"What?"

"Yeah, Cathy, Leah followed me there and confronted me, and I had to be honest with her, so she gave me my ring back. Because she knows that my future is with Jasmine and Jordan, but I feel bad that she got hurt."

"And she only asked one thing of us, and that's to let people think that she called off the wedding when she found out that I have a child. And anybody who knows her will believe it because she's always been extremely vocal about not wanting to marry a man with a kid. So please, don't tell anyone otherwise because that's the least I can do for her."

"Julian, of course, we won't tell anyone. You already know that I didn't think she was right for you, but I do care about her, and I never wanted her to get hurt."

"Cathy, I know that, and I'm pretty sure that Leah knows it too. And believe it or not, she's at my house with Jasmine packing up her things."

"What? Did I hear you right?"

"Yeah, dad, they were over there together, but Jasmine texted a few minutes ago and should be here any minute now."

"Well, I would like to have been a fly on the wall to hear what they were talking about."

"They're okay, and she ate lunch with us at Jasmine's yesterday."

Just then, the doorbell rang, and I got up quickly to answer it. And Jasmine was standing there looking like a vision of pure beauty.

'Hey, babe, I missed you." Reaching out, I hugged her as she walked in.

"I missed you too."

Closing the door quickly, I leaned in to kiss her, only to hear the sound of people clearing their throats, so we looked in that direction to see my family approaching us smiling, as they reached out to embrace her, and I stepped to the side."

" I've missed you all so much. And I'm sorry that I kept Jordan away from you guys, but at the time, I didn't have a choice."

"Jasmine, we all need to focus on the present and future, not on the past. Under the circumstances, your family did what they felt was right for everybody involved. And we love that beautiful, smart little girl already because she's extraordinary like her mom."

Tears were lapping down her face, "Mrs. Allison, you can't possibly imagine what those words mean to me. I love you all."

"Sweetie, we love you too."

After many hugs, Jasmine and I went upstairs to check on Jordan, who was still sound asleep, so we went back downstairs to talk with my family, and it felt as though we'd never been apart.

When we finally made it home, we talked about getting married soon, although we didn't want to hurt Leah. But we needed to get married before people started doing the math once they found out about Jordan, and we were wondering if we were married before word got out, if she could be summoned and forced to testify against me.

The following day, I called Pete, told him about Jordan, and that Jasmine and I were back together. And we needed to know if we were married if I could still be charged with statutory rape once the story broke?

After the initial shock wore off following about ten minutes of silence, he said no, and encouraged us to get married immediately. Because otherwise, it could become an issue for me, and the best way to safeguard myself and my family would be to get married quickly and discreetly.

And later that day, it was on-line and on the local news that the wedding of the year between Julian Alexander Peterson and Leah Marie Jones had been called off, but no further details were available as of yet, but to stay tuned. So we needed to move swiftly.

If we stayed here right now, there would be no way to prevent everything from coming out because our families are very prominent and high profile in our community. And I didn't want to harm my family's company because my great grandparents had worked too long and too hard for me to damage their legacy with this type of scandal. People wouldn't care that we were in love then and still are. They'd see me as a man who took advantage of a young girl, and it ended in a pregnancy. And they'd see me as being cruel by hurting Leah and marrying someone else so quickly.

We had the option of moving to Seattle, but Jasmine's parents were considering moving back here, and we wanted Jordan to be near both sets of her grandparents and her aunt. There were also a lot of our other family members on both sides who resided nearby.

So we decided to get married within the next two weeks in Seattle and perhaps live there for a year. Because with technology, I didn't necessarily have to be in Richmond to do my work. I could work from home, like Jasmine.

But, we wanted to tell Leah first because it would be one week before our wedding would've taken place, and it was vital for us to explain to her why because we owed her that much.

Telling her wouldn't be easy, but it had to happen because it was the right thing to do. Because even though we wouldn't be getting married here, she might still find out and be upset that we got married so soon. So I phoned and asked if we could come over to talk because we didn't want to take the chance of the three of us being seen or photographed at a restaurant or somewhere in public together. Because if everything

came out now, this definitely wouldn't help our case.
We'd come off as being cold and callous.

She agreed, and when we went there, things started
quite awkwardly because I had a few personal items
that she'd boxed up and pretty much shoved in my chest
as we walked in. So I took the box to the car while
Jasmine stayed, and I took a minute or two to clear my
head.

Returning inside, I saw Jasmine seated at the kitchen
table, and Leah was handing her a glass of tea. And
she'd also poured a glass for herself and one for me as
well.

I went and took a seat, and Leah sat down too.

"So, what do you all want to talk to me about? Because
if you're wondering, I haven't told anyone what
happened. I just said that I'd called off the wedding, as I
said I would, but that's all I've disclosed to anyone so
far. I haven't even told my parents about Jordan yet. I
simply said that I'd changed my mind, and my mom
helped me with the cancellations without asking a lot of
questions. Julian, I told you that I wouldn't mention
Jasmine's age, and I won't. So you don't have to worry
about that."

"I know, and I appreciate it, but our concern is that it's
going to come out eventually anyway. So we want to tell

you about our plans and explain to you why we're doing
this?"

"Okay, I'm listening, and then I need to tell y'all about a
decision that I've made as well." Turning toward me, she
looked at me intently.

"Alright, well, you already know that I could've and
probably would've been charged with statutory rape
years ago if officials had known about Jasmine's
pregnancy. So I talked to an attorney to see if I could
still be charged and prosecuted now, and he said yes.
And that the only way to safeguard me against it would
be for us to get married immediately, so Jasmine
couldn't be summoned as a witness and forced to testify
against me."

"Yeah, that has crossed my mind too, and I don't want
anything to happen to you, so I understand. And I
appreciate hearing it from you all myself. So when's the
big wedding?" Tears were lapping down her face and
Jasmine's too.

"Leah, we're not having a big wedding because we'd
never do that to you. It's going to be a simple ceremony
two weeks from now in Seattle with just our immediate
families and two or three other people present.
Honestly, it's going to be so simple that we haven't even
told them yet. And Julian and I are going to live there for
a year before we move back here. We want to show
respect for you and your family and to let all of this

hopefully blow over. Because we don't want to hurt anybody."

"Sighing, she reached for Jasmine's hand, "Thank you for showing me what it means to be selfless and for forcing me to reevaluate some things about myself. I don't know if Julian has mentioned this to you or not, but I have a standing job offer in New York, where I once resided. So, I'm going to take it, and I think it'll be good for me." Clearing her throat, she let go of her hand.

"Leah, I wish you a lifetime of happiness, and I hope that we can all be friends someday."

"Yeah, Jasmine, I think I'd like that too."

When we got ready to leave, Leah and I embraced, " I hope you know that I never meant to hurt you, and I'll always care about you and your happiness. And I want you to find someone truly deserving of you. Please tell me you know that."

"Yeah, I do know that, and I'll always care about you too, and I want to find what you and Jasmine share because I want a love that can withstand time, distance, heartache, and tears and never skip a beat. You two are fated and destined to be together, and that's a good thing."

As soon as we broke our embrace, she and Jasmine hugged, "Leah, I haven't known you for long, and we

met under crazy circumstances, but I want you to be
happy. And I hope that we can, at the very least, text
each other occasionally and keep in touch. I know you
said that you're selfish, but the way you've handled this
situation has been anything but that."

On our way home, we discussed our simple ceremony.
And we decided that we'd go over to my parents later,
so we could skype with hers' and fill everyone in on our
plans.

That evening, sitting down with my family and Brian at
the kitchen table, we pulled up Jasmine's family on
zoom, and we told them what our plans were, much to
everyone's delight. And we included our grandparents.

Two days later, we flew back to Seattle and made plans
for our simple wedding that would take place at home in
a candlelight ceremony. And it would be witnessed by
our parents, grandparents, Cathy, and her boyfriend if
he was back from an overseas business trip in time,
along with Ms.Granger and her husband. And of course,
I had to invite my boy, Pete, and his girl, Megan.

My family flew in several days before the ceremony, and
it was like joyous Christmas and birthday celebrations
from years gone by. It didn't feel as though we'd ever
been apart because the foundation of our family
dynamic was and always will be love. A love that
allowed for transgressions overflowed with
understanding and forgiveness and never changed.

On the day before our wedding, I stayed at the hotel, where I'd previously booked a room because Jasmine didn't want me to see her until she was walking down the stairs towards me. Megan stayed at the house with Jasmine and our families so that Pete could stay with me; therefore, I like that girl.

"Hey, bruh, I can't tell you how happy I am that you and Jasmine have found each other again. And not only did you find her, but you also found out that you're the father of a beautiful little girl who looks just like you. Jordan looks like you spit her out. And there were moments that I thought you were just banging your head against a brick wall, hoping to reunite with Jasmine. But I'm glad I was proven wrong. Not to mention that I'm getting a goddaughter out the deal."

"Now, I think it's time for us to finish our last beer and turn in early because tomorrow night is your wedding night. And I'm sure you want to be well-rested to make up for all the time you guys have been apart. You all will be knocking boots like crazy! And bruh, try not to throw your back out because she's not going anywhere! She's here to stay!" Laughing loudly, as we fist-bumped, I laughed too.

"Yeah, yeah, why is everything always about sex with you?'

"Hey, that's because when it's with the one you love, there's no better feeling in the world. I get excited just thinking about how good it feels!"

"Picking up my beer bottle, I tilted it toward him, and he did likewise, "So I think my boy has found the one."

"Yeah, I have found her because Megan is my heart. And like I told you before, my whorish ways are over! Having sex is different than making love, and I by far prefer the latter."

Chapter 11

The next day, Pete and I went downstairs to have lunch at the hotel restaurant, as I anxiously counted down the time to go home. Because I was about to marry the love of my life and unite my family, and my next order of business would be to change Jordan's last name from Kennedy to Peterson.

When the time finally came for us to go over to the house, my heart was bursting with happiness. So, I didn't feel nervous at all! I was just ready to say I do for a lifetime.

Opening the door quietly, Pete and I entered, and I was astonished at how the house now looked like a lovely wedding venue. All the family room furniture had been rearranged and strategically placed to accommodate tall white chairs with red sashes fastened elegantly with big silver pendants. There were also tall silver vases with long-stemmed red roses everywhere, along with tall silver candlesticks holding fragrant red candles. There were even silver bows all over the staircase. It looked stunning, and I was amazed that all of this had taken place in such a short time frame.

"Hey, guys. Julian, your mom, and everybody else is upstairs and said to keep you guys down here until the ceremony starts. So, you all are to get dressed in the downstairs bedroom. And son, you look happy."

"Yeah, dad, I am because today is a day that I've dreamed of for far too long, and now it's about to come true."

"Alright, well, you guys need to go get ready because the ceremony will be starting soon, and I'll come to get you all to take your places. Oh, yeah, Brian flew in earlier today, so he's here.'

"Okay, cool, I'm glad he made it."

Pete and I got dressed, and it wasn't long before my father came to get us, and we took our places along with the officiant in front of a silver backdrop with our initials in fancy red letters.

Looking incredibly proud and happy, my parents and Mrs. Carla came in along with our grandparents and took their seats along with Ms. Granger, her husband, and Brian. And our photographer was taking pictures.

And to my pleasant surprise, Megan started to sing beautifully the lyrics from a love song that Jasmine and I had slow- danced to years ago, saying it was our song. So at that moment, I could feel the enormous weight of my love for her bearing down on me because she is my endless love. And Jordan is the product of our love for each other.

But then, I looked up and saw Cathy, who was walking down the stairs wearing a pretty long silver dress with a red sash, followed by my little princess wearing a red dress and carrying a silver basket throwing out red rose petals as she walked. And when she descended the stairs, she put in great effort to make her dress twirl along with her long hair that was hanging in loose curls, much to the delight of us all. She looked adorable, and I could feel my heart swelling with pride as she went and stood beside Cathy.

Megan finished her song, and a recording of the wedding march started playing. And Jasmine and her father appeared at the top of the stairs, and I teared up when I saw her dressed in a simple but stunning white gown with a crystal and silver belt and thin silver and crystal straps. Her hair was in soft curls, and she looked stunning with an exquisite silver headpiece, carrying a bouquet of petite red roses.

As they slowly descended the stairs, her father walked her to me, kissed her on the cheek, stepped back, and took a seat next to Ms. Carla. And the rest of that momentous occasion is a blur because the next thing I knew, the officiant was saying that I could kiss my beautiful bride. And our families were squealing with delight because, with those words, we had become one family. As we stood there and kissed, Jordan came and wrapped her arms around our legs and squeezed tightly.

Our lobster dinner was good, and in the midst of that, Pete stood up to make a toast, " Hey guys, as we all know, Jasmine is without a doubt, the love of Julian's life. And now that he's found her again, I won't have to use a tranquilizer gun on him to stop him from looking for her. And I'm thrilled to witness not only their unity but his family's unity because he's the father of a beautiful little girl, who's the spitting image of him. So, my brother here's to a lifetime of happiness for you and your family. Here, here."

Chuckling, everyone took a sip of champagne as Jasmine, and I leaned in and kissed gently, and Jordan covered her eyes.

"Then, Cathy stood, "Well, Jasmine and I grew up like sisters, and today, I can proudly say that we are. And I couldn't be prouder of my beautiful little niece who does indeed look just like her father, but she luckily acts like her mother. Here, here."

Laughing loudly, as she held up her glass, everyone else did too. We all sipped good champagne, and Jordan drank sparkling apple juice.

Later that night, after we'd cut our wedding cake and danced the night away, our parents kept Jordan. While we flew on my father's plan to San Francisco, California, for a five-day honeymoon at the Catamaran Resort Hotel and spa, by the same pilot who had flown me to Seattle, and he was extremely happy for us. We would've stayed longer, but we were both anxious to get back to our daughter and start our life as a family.

Our hotel accommodations were spectacular, and we enjoyed every moment of our time together, with an enormous amount of it spent lounging in a massive heart-shaped bed. We also relished romantic dinners on the balcony and slow-dancing in the resorts' ballroom. Our honeymoon was a joyous time that we will never forget, and we took tons of pictures to look back on and show our daughter someday.

And time and tide march on because we were so happy and caught up in the joy of being a family that before we knew it, a year had passed, and we were moving to our brand new home in Richmond. I'd sold our old house furnishings and all because I wanted us to have a fresh start. I wanted Jasmine to have a home that no other woman had ever stayed at or cooked in her kitchen. And thankfully, I could afford to give her that. And our house in Seattle sold quickly, so the new owners will be moving in as soon as we vacate. But first, we had to travel to Japan again as a family for Jasmine's company that was rapidly expanding. And we'd use the opportunity once again to teach Jordan about other cultures and traditions.

My in-laws were also moving because they'd decided to wait until we could all move back home together. They couldn't bear to be away from Jordan, and I, of all people, certainly understood that. Because this beautiful, amazing little girl brings us all great joy. So much so that my family and Brian have flown to Seattle numerous times over the past year. Jordan adores them, as they do her. Pete and Megan have joined them on occasion and are now engaged. And Cathy and Bryan are hanging tight, and something tells me that he's in the picture to stay. So, I wouldn't be surprised if she's showing us a ring sometime soon.

And we're incredibly excited that we'll have a wedding to attend, in less than a month, after our move home because we've kept in touch with Leah. So she's invited us to her wedding to Thomas, being held at a ritzy country club in the spring, and we are thrilled for her, well, actually for them.

She told Jasmine that it was because of her that she'd reevaluated her decision to break things off with him simply because he has a child. So once she moved back to New York, they realized that there were still some residual feelings there. Eventually, they started hanging out and fell in love all over again. And that does my heart a world of good because not only have I found my destiny, but she's found hers.